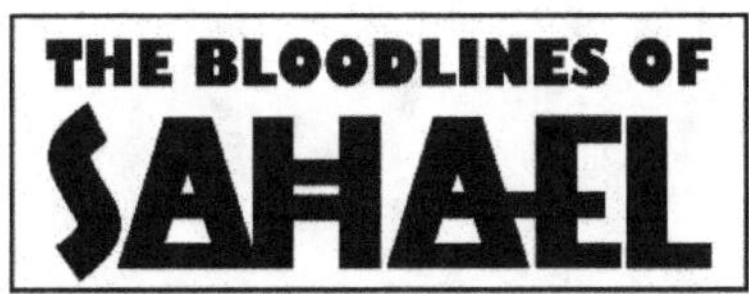

VOLUME TWO

BOOK THREE

THE BATTLE FOR IFF

BY

DWAYNE ANTHONY MADRY

Printed in the United States of America

First Printing, 2025

Cover Design by JessHavok

ISBN 978-1-963089-39-4

www.SAHAEL.com

Intoduction into Sahael

In the heart of the desert Sandlands, a storm brewed—not of sand and wind, but of fury and determination. Aamira stood at the forefront of an epic confrontation, locked in a battle for the very soul of her people. The forces that had occupied IFF were relentless, their eyes set on routing her and the remnants of the sacred bloodline, an ancient lineage destined to reclaim their rightful place in the world. They sought to extinguish the flame of hope that flickered within her, but Aamira was no ordinary adversary; she was the embodiment of a prophecy long whispered in the shadows. With the knowledge she had unlocked—the secrets of ages past—Aamira wielded wisdom as her sword. Each revelation was a spark that ignited her resolve, fueling her purpose to lead her people to safety and reclaim their heritage. The prophecy spoke of a time when the sacred bloodline would rise against the encroaching darkness, and now, that time had come.

As the sun set behind the jagged peaks, casting an ominous glow over the battlefield, Aamira rallied her kin, their hearts beating as one. She was their beacon, a symbol of resilience in the face of overwhelming odds. With the echoes of their ancestors urging them on, they prepared to confront the invaders, who threatened to sever the ties that bound them to their past and future. The clash of steel rang out like thunder across the desert, a cacophony of defiance against tyranny. Aamira fought with the ferocity of a mother Bear, her every strike infused with purpose, each movement choreographed by the whispers of the prophecy. She felt the pulse of the land beneath her feet, guiding her, empowering her to protect not just her people, but the very essence of IFF itself. As the battle raged, Aamira harnessed the ancient knowledge she had uncovered, weaving it into her strategy. She called upon the spirits of the earth, summoning the strength of the sacred bloodline to bolster her allies. Together, they became an unstoppable force, a tide of hope and courage against the relentless onslaught of their oppressors.

In the midst of chaos, Aamira glimpsed the horizon—the distant silhouette of SAHAEL, a promise of safety and sanctuary. She knew that if they could withstand this onslaught, if they could push through the darkness, they could reclaim their destiny and forge a new beginning. The battle for IFF was not just a fight for land; it was a fight for identity, for culture, for the very soul of her people. This was their moment—a turning point in a saga that would echo through the ages. The Battle for IFF was not just a clash of swords; it was a declaration of existence, a fight to reclaim their narrative from the annals of history. And as Aamira stood tall amidst the chaos, she knew that this was only the beginning of their extraordinary journey, a journey that would lead them to SAHAEL and beyond, where legends are forged and destinies fulfilled.

CHAPTER CONTENTS

CHAPTER I
THE AWAKENING OF THE BLOODLINE

The Desert Sand Lands of IFF, Cheops Pyramid

The war had ended.

Karnak was safe.

Yet, as Aamira awoke the morning after returning to the hidden city, nausea gripped her stomach. Her sons were safe, yes, but thousands had died, and her marriage was faltering.

She glanced at Abioye asleep next to her. His devotion to his mother had nearly torn them apart, and resentment now festered in Aamira's chest.

The nausea continued.

She quietly left the bed and dressed, exiting the spacious royal chambers with their green and purple curtains blocking the view of Karnak below.

She needed council, which meant she needed to find Educator Adewara, her mentor.

The streets of Karnak were quiet this early in the morning,

with only a handful of merchants waving to their queen. Most people slept after the celebration of the night before…those who weren't mourning the loss of loved ones in the battle with General Scipio.

Aamira entered Cheops Pyramid and ascended the main steps, entering the cavernous library with its stacks of weathered parchment and brass plated records. Adewara sat as he usually did in the main chamber, pouring over histories and maps. His graying beard seemed to remain perpetually the same length, with few wrinkles on his dark skin. He seemed almost ageless.

"You're finally here good," Adewara said.

"The sun hasn't even fully risen," Aamira replied as she sat across from him at the sandstone table. "You expected me here earlier?"

Adewara smiled and sat back. "After the events of the last few days, I figured you would want to talk sooner as opposed to later. Much has happened. Your young boys fought well according to their commanders."

"The triplets are ten years old," Aamira said, blowing a breath from her nose. "They shouldn't be fighting in a war at all."

"And yet children their age are slaves, working the fields all day, or being raped by wicked owners with impunity. You and your sons are meant to stop that. Don't forget your calling, Aamira. As a princess of Sahael, you will help usher in a new world for black people across Aarde. For all people, truly."

"I understand," Aamira said. She had been hearing this since her first meeting with the prophet Solomon well over a decade ago. For now, she didn't need a recap. She needed answers. "I have a lot of questions, like who were those collectors of dead bodies we saw after the battle?"

"They're known as the Ennead, who are being led by

Second Commander Geb of the second Ennead Legion," Adewara confirmed. "The Ennead can't hear Nova's song. You'll remember the music we heard on the air. Normally only the Demirrian priests can hear it when collecting bodies. I don't know why we could hear it, but the Ennead definitely can't because of their service to the dark Lord Commander Natas. They employ half-dead Nethani priests who can hear Nova's song."

"According to what I've learned, aren't the Demirrians responsible for retrieving the dead?" Aamira asked. "Also, aren't the Demirrians the ones who can hear Nova's song?"

Adewara nodded his head. "Yes, but again, we heard the song too. I can't explain why it's happening. To find out more about this phenomenon we need more information. The Ennead are taking the bodies back to Naharis's realm for reasons beyond my understanding. We need to get to Sahael to find the answers we'll need. Only then will the heavens open and knowledge be poured out on our heads."

Sitting back in her chair, images flooded Aamira's mind of the white mist billowing from the dead bodies on the battlefield and the terrifying way they writhed and contorted before the Ennead arrived in the portals.

"After I killed General Scipio," Aamira said slowly, "the blanket of whiteness appeared several inches above the sea of dead bodies. The dead started breathing and inhaling and exhaling the mist. What was that fog? What does it portend?"

"I don't know." Adewara rubbed his forehead. "I know you and Abioye think we Educators have all the answers, but it seems to me that since your arrival on IFF, when the quakes started almost 12 years ago now, the Signs of the Times began, and my understanding has been stretched to its limits."

"How did this mist of whiteness get here in the first place?"

Aamira asked.

"No one knows," Adewara said. "At least no one in the library of Timbuktu where I studied. All I can tell you is that Second Commander Geb or Natas' inner circle is looking for you and will not stop looking for you until he finds you, your children and any Navigators left alive. That was why I pulled you out of there so quickly once I realized what was going on. If any Ennead high priests had exited one of the portals, they would have known instantly you were a princess of Sahael. Their power is unknown. They would have summoned Geb or even Natas himself. We were in no position for that type of attention."

"What about the portals?" Aamira asked. "We've studied the Nairohenge Gates and their ability to transport people to other gates across Aarde, but these were independent portals untethered to a gate."

"The portals are known as Nebuchadnezzar's portals. Second Commander Geb wears one of Njiru's Chalcedony rings that allows him the ability to open the Chalcedony portals. More than one portal opened, so I'm betting the other commanders of Natas were together allowing the Ennead to go through before they themselves set foot on the battlefield. That's when I knew that the Demirrian's had lost the ability to retrieve and bring the dead back to their homelands to be buried."

"Wait!" Aamira said. "Are Njiru's rings on our fingers the same type of rings that can open up portals?"

Nodding his head, Adewara reached across the table and grabbed a goblet full of juice and took a drink. "Yes, they are, but yours and Abioye's are dormant for reasons I do not know. Yet another mystery that can be figured out when you return to Sahael."

"Nothing can be straightforward in life, can it?" Aamira

grabbed Adewara's cup and took a drink as well. The Amarula was strong. "We have hard to understand prophecies; General Scipio has hard to understand prophecies apparently too. Prophecies on top of prophecies, and no one knows exactly what the mean or how to interpret them until after they happen."

Adewara smiled playfully. "It's as Nyikang predicted. His prophecy stated that before the fall of Sahael, there would be an invasion to prevent Sahael from using the Nairohenge Gates. The ancient Kemites, Sahael, Egyptus, and Horn approved after hearing Nyikang's prophecy and approved them and many others to travel in secret to the outer lands to build secondary civilizations, ensuring Sahael's house would prevent it from happening. Nyikang was of Egyptian descent and built Cheops pyramid below the city of Karnak knowing the Yoruban people would need refuge before being called back to reclaim their homeland and kingdom."

"Great, more prophecies," Aamira breathed, taking another drink of the strong wine. "Knowing more about this Nyikang woman would be helpful."

"Nyikang was a man," Adewara corrected.

"I'll listen to his prophecy then," Aamira grinned. "Not all men are smarter than women anyway, so I'm assuming his prophecy is easier to understand, and probably more accurate."

"He was an Egyptian ordered by the Ptolemies and Pharaohs to come to Sahael and get others to come with him so a remnant of the Yoruban bloodline would be able to return to Sahael at the chosen times. He prophesied that Naki's flame would restore every Yoruban to their natural immortal state. Nyikang's purpose was to save the Yorubans that were being hunted for sport, putting them in different cities until their awakening took place. That was when you arrived, triggering the Signs of the Times and inadvertently forcing the Yoruban bloodline to return to Cheops Pyramid."

Aamira held the goblet high. "See? Now that's a prophecy you can point to that worked out just as it was written. To Nyikang who was probably raised by his sister for his clear prophecy!" Aamira drank the rest of the wine in tribute to Nyikang.

Chuckling, Adewara leaned forward. "Nyikang saw a vision of the Yoruban people being transported here in obsidian cages to be hunted for sport and wiped out systematically, by the Lord Commander Natas' Dalean Generals."

"Now I understand why they're considered the Diaspora," Aamira said.

"Indeed, when the Narsans dropped the Yorubans here on the Desert Sand Lands of IFF, they thought they were displacing a people to a continent they knew nothing about as Diaspora. The Narsans knew about Nyikang's prophecy. Lord Commander Natas thought they were placing your people in another home they knew nothing about, not realizing Nyikang had been here from the beginning."

"They'd been here all along waiting to be redeemed and saved?" Aamira asked.

"Yes," Adewara confirmed. "The chosen bloodlines, under the direction of the ancient Kemites, created failsafe mechanisms in Sahael designed to restrict movements of the four realms if Sahael was overrun."

"We all know Sahael was made uninhabitable by these failsafes," Aamira said. "Not exactly the smartest way to do things if no one can ever live there again. It's like burning down your house so robbers can't get in."

"There's more to it than that," Adewara continued. "To activate HÉAS's shield is to protect every inhabitant of Aarde that will one day return to Alkebulan for safety, refuge, and comfort. If you'd like to know more about HÉAS's shield, you have to find out more in Sahael," Adewara said.

"Of course," Aamira said, shaking her head. "You can't learn how to save Sahael until you're inside Sahael. That sounds about right. In any case, we have a way to travel without exposing ourselves or the Yoruban people. We can use the Nibiru Tunnels. It will keep the Ennead focused on the dead ensuring all of us are safe. Before that though, tell me what you can about HÉAS's shield."

Adewara reached over and pulled a leatherbound book from the far side of the table. The dry pages crinkled as he opened it. "The Orichalcum that grows in Sahael will grow forever, producing unlimited amounts. It also holds unlimited power that can only be controlled by the four bloodline families that operate the four kingdoms and reside in Khartoum Palace. When the kingdom was divided because of petty squabbles that eventually led to the downfall of the capital city of Sahael, the Orichalcum was merely a strong metal. So long as there is unity, Sahael cannot fall, even to Natas."

"I can see why Solomon went through all he did to meet with Oadira, Heziara, Damisiah, and myself; even then when we arrive, we'll need to be directed to know what needs to be done next," Aamira said. "Why is the Orichalcum so powerful when there is unity?"

"Spiritual energy of all four bloodlines will be required to save Aarde. That spiritual energy is focused by the Orichalcum. The Blood of the Ancients, the Sacred Blood, the Divine Blood, and the Cursed Blood will be essential to saving our souls. The Ancient Kemites built mechanisms to prevent what happened to their world Kolob from happening here in Aarde. In order to create HÉAS's shield, all four realms need to be maintained by all four bloodlines. The four bloodlines are needed in Horn, Alkebulan, Egypt, and Sahael."

"What are the mechanisms you mentioned? Are they machines, or something spiritual, since that's what's needed to power the Orichalcum?" Aamira asked.

"The mechanisms were put in place hidden below the ground by our ancient ancestors. They are Neimoidia orbital defense lasers hidden below Neolithic's chamber located in each of the four realms, Sahael, Egyptus and Horn."

"Wait, what?" Aamira questioned. "Lasers hidden underground? Like the myth of the fire breathers from the old children's stories? None of that is real. You're talking about mythic machines that can focus flame."

Adewara stared at Aamira for a moment. "The spiritual and physical are always tied together. When one is at its zenith, the other will follow. Under the ancient Kemites, knowledge was as pure as glacial water. Technologies you cannot understand were created. It was only through pride and unbelief that they were lost to the world."

"If these lasers exist," Aamira continued warily, "then why weren't they used during Natas' attack 30 years ago?"

"Because the bloodlines weren't united. Yes, your parents, and the parents of your cousins, had bonded and lived in the palaces, but the people were still divided and distrustful of one another. The knowledge had not been restored because of this division. They will all be needed to help support and save Aarde."

Aamira scratched behind her ear. If she hadn't experienced everything over the past decade, she would have been more skeptical. Still, it was a lot to take in.

"Is there a way to determine how all of these bloodlines are connected?" she asked. "I've looked around this library and haven, but I haven't seen any records that contain the information I've been looking for."

"Indeed," Adewara said as he flipped through the pages in one of Nyikang's Nalace journals. "I have what you've been looking for. What I have here is a detailed history of the sacred bloodlines prior to the invasion of Sahael. There are six sacred bloodlines; the Oralian bloodline, the Astorian bloodline, the Eagalian bloodline, the Lysinnian bloodline, and lastly, the Rysallian bloodline.

"You said six but only named five," Aamira said.

Adewara pointed at a genealogical chart with names and branching lineages like tree limbs. "The Lysinnian bloodline was split into two, the Egyptian Bloodline and the Horn bloodline. These sacred tribes were a part of the ancient order in Aarde. The Oralian tribe would later become the Orishan tribe, The Astorian tribe would later become the Yoruban tribe, the Eagalian tribe would later become the Hausan Tribe, and the Lysinnian tribe would later become the Egyptian and the Horn bloodline. The six of them were chosen by Obatala and Ishtar, who selected the Lysinnians as keepers of the sacred six bloodlines."

A side branch broke off from the rest on the page with the symbol of the Rysallians. Aamira tapped it with her finger. "What about these Rysallians? Why aren't they even mentioned? What can you tell us about them?"

"You have a lot of questions this morning," Adewara smiled. He seemed energized, but Aamira knew him well enough to see the fatigue in his eyes. "To sum it up for you," Adewara continued, "Ishtar and Obatala wanted to use them as agents of the order. Their responsibility was to infiltrate due to their witan skin to help keep the other eleven bloodlines from being enslaved. Before the great divines could inform of their intentions, they started to rebel and wanted the right to control Aarde and make things their way. The witans had grown rich and powerful in this time, creating in their hearts a cultural predisposition towards control and fear. The great divines knew this as well and wanted to use the witans for that purpose."

"So, what happened?" Aamira asked.

"War." Adewara stood and motioned for Aamira to follow him. Another wave of nausea hit her, and she swayed for a moment.

"Are you alright, Aamira?" Adewara asked, taking her arm to steady her.

"I just got up too quickly. I felt nauseous for a second. I'm fine."

They walked around a bookshelf toward Nephrophida's Interactive map hanging on the wall in an alcove. Adewara pointed to the land of Inheritance, where the skirmish took place.

"The Chosen bloodlines forced the Rysallians, into isolation after creating the Ancient Order. As a result, they chose to live in Western Aarde. They stayed away from Eastern Aarde and were the only witan bloodline apart of the six sacred bloodlines, the Nine divine bloodlines, and the chosen bloodlines."

"And after all this time in Western Aarde, I'm sure they thrived," Aamira said.

Nodding, Adewara leaned against a sandstone pillar. "Indeed, after living in isolation in Western Aarde, the Rysallian bloodline conquered all the Western tribes. They subjected everyone in Western Aarde to their way of life. There was nothing the Watchers could do except focus on Eastern Aarde. Sahael lost contact with the Rysallians, the three realms knew they were lost and that there was no way they could save the enslaved inhabitants due to the Nibiru Wall that separated them." Adewara pointed to the image of a long wall running thousands of miles on the map between the eastern and western halves.

"So, the Rysallian enslaved all of western Aarde?" Aamira asked.

"Yes," Adewara replied.

"It's hard to grasp why the Rysallians wanted to enslave a group of their own people despite their similarities," Aamira said.

"I'm tired," Adewara admitted. "Let's go back and sit."

The two of them returned to the stone table and sat once again. Adewara rubbed his eyes and took a deep breath.

"There are two great cancers that infect humanity," he spoke, eyes locked on Aamira. "You, my queen, suffer from one, though you hold it at bay."

"And what is that?" Aamira asked.

"Anger. The other is a lust for control, which thankfully has not infected you. These cancers spread in entire cultures. It happens among the witans. It happened in Sahael. When anger and control meet, devastation and slavery follow. Something happened among the Rysallians that allowed these cancers to flourish. I've heard it was due to the color of the skin of the chosen order. There was a slight difference in their skin colors, the lighter skinned seeing themselves as superior to the darker skinned, and thus having lighter brown skin justified them in taking out their anger and aggression on their brothers. There are black people on the other side of the Nibiru Wall which are being enslaved against their will and denied their freedoms because of their skin color, just like in the colonies."

"Why didn't Sahael do anything to prevent any of this from happening when they were at the peak of their power?" Aamira asked.

"As I've said before, Sahael lost all contact and communication," Adewara answered. "And Sahael itself was divided. The Narsans took control of the Nibiru Gates and the Nibiru Wall. There was no way to help them when Sahael fell. The Nairohenge gates retracted into the grounds throughout Western Aarde, preventing interference from Sahael, Egypt, and Horn. These Nairohenge Gates were made of Orichalcum and were dotted across Aarde. Imagine fifteen doors encapsulated in a circle created to puncture the landmass, with four singular gates in the center. These Gates were created by Nairo, an ancient Kemite who was ordered by Kainoa and Kaimana to create a means of travel for the Kemettian people to help them avoid the sun by any means necessary."

"This Orichalcum that the Nairohenge Gates are made out of has the same spiritual properties you mentioned, right?" Aamira asked, starting to put things together.

"Yes, it's a material not from Aarde but is foreign," Adewara said. "You remember in the center of Nephrophida's Interactive map there was the impact site of a large asteroid known as Nyathera's asteroid. It punctured Aarde's atmosphere, breaking into various pieces that hit all over Aarde and in various spots in the large bodies of water. The largest chunk of Nyathera's asteroid crashed down in what is now called Sahael, Egypt, and Horn. The ancient Kemites emerging from Nyathera's asteroid in ancient white spacesuits. It made the continent of Alkebulan a choice land above all other lands in Aarde. The Orichalcum from Nyathera's asteroid helped them build Nairohenge Gates all over Aarde so that the Ancient Kemites could move freely throughout the world. The ancients remained in Sahael but disappeared from Horn and Egypt. That is where their history ends. It seems as if we need to get to Sahael to find out more. The records said that once the four Pharaohs are found, then Egypt and Horn can be brought back into the fold to help Sahael."

Adewara closed the book and stood.

"I need some sleep. It's been a long couple days. How are you and Abioye after everything with Adana?"

"I don't know," Aamira admitted. "Strained."

"You look pale. How are you feeling?"

"The battle took a lot out of me. Plus, I woke up feeling a bit sick. I'll be fine."

Adewara looked her up and down, nodding his head. "You and Abioye must come to terms with many things. You are at a crossroad. Change is coming unexpectedly. You must face it together, or all will be lost."

He turned and walked away, leaving Aamira alone in the pyramid. What changes did he speak of? She stood and again felt her stomach protest. What changes could possibly be greater than what they currently faced?

It didn't matter. She would face them, alone if necessary.

Aamira soon discovered the changes Adewara inferred.

She was pregnant.

Abioye was overjoyed, but Aamira felt conflicted. Distance existed between her and Abioye, a distance that grew every day, though he seemed unaware.

Months passed and her baby developed inside her. The quakes that had been so common since her arrival on IFF worsened, creating more death in the area. Several buildings collapsed, killing dozens of Karnak citizens. The situation in the sandstone city became tenuous at best. Fear spread.

In the skies overhead, Narsan airships appeared regularly, searching for more dead to collect. They never entered the city, whether it was hidden from their view, or some other force kept them at bay, Aamira didn't know. The time to leave Karnak was quickly approaching, as was the birth of her fourth child.

When the day finally arrived, Aamira gave birth to a strong and healthy baby boy. Abioye wanted to name the child after his father, but Aamira had been told the boy's name in a dream: Yinká, meaning 'surround me.' What that portended, Aamira could only guess.

Several days after the birth, Adewara requested to speak with the king and queen. He entered the royal residence and bowed.

"I have found a Navigator among our people," Adewara smiled. "She served in the old court as a youth and trained in the use of not only the tunnels, but Nairohenge Gates as well. Should we find a Gate at any time on our journey, she will be invaluable in being able to use it. Before departing Cheops pyramid for good with the Yoruban people, the Navigator shared with me what I already knew about the Nairohenge Gates. I feel that this knowledge is important for you to know and the danger the Nairohenge Gate pose as a threat to Aarde if not properly controlled and managed by Sahael. If a fallen Sahael is to rise from the ashes to glory once again, understanding the Nairohenge Gates will be vital. Once you are able, I would invite both of you to come to the pyramid for a lesson. Do you agree?"

"Yes!" Abioye replied enthusiastically.

Aamira merely nodded as she held her baby close.

Lessons and history. She had to know it all, but for some reason here with her newborn, she wanted nothing more than to take her children and disappear into the desert.

"I will be there," she mumbled.

There would be no disappearing today.

CHAPTER II
THE NAIROHENGE GATES

Cheops Pyramid

A warm breeze blew down the corridor leading to the stone table in the center of Cheops Pyramid. The summer heat radiated even here underground. Sweat clung to Aamira's clothing. Her body hurt from the birth less than a week before. Worse than that, she felt emotionally drained. Being here with Adewara the Educator and her kingly husband Abioye did nothing to tilt it one way or the other. She knew Adewara was doing what he thought best, since the time to leave the safety of Karnak rapidly approached, but she still had no desire to be here. And her growing resentment for Abioye only seemed accented by the need to be in proximity with one another.

"Welcome and thanks for coming, King and Queen Adesola," Adewara began. He stood where he normally did during their education sessions, in front of the table with sets of metal plated records before him; a black slated board behind covered in maps. "I understand we are getting ready to depart and leave this place. The council voted yesterday, pending your ratification, to leave a small group behind to keep Karnak running. There is worry about the stability of the buildings with the quakes intensifying, but the pyramid itself is safe, so they will reside here and care for everything else as best they can.”

Aamira nodded, only half listening. Staying behind didn't sound so bad. Maybe she could give her responsibilities for the Yoruban people to someone else and live here in Karnak until the end of the world.

“What I share with you must stay with the Royal family of the sacred bloodline,” Adewara continued, oblivious to Aamira's inner monologue. “This is information that must remain confidential and classified forever. Aamira, Abioye, it will be your duty to explain it to your sons Yekú, Yemí, Yomí, and baby Yinká when the time is right. They are young, but this knowledge belongs to them as well.”

Footsteps echoed from the corridor and Aamira turned to see a woman in gray and purple robes approaching. Streaks of gray weaved through her dreadlocks, stretching to the small of her back, with braids and designs throughout her hair like a labyrinth. She was strong, with an athletic chiseled frame, and Ivory teeth. She looked powerful and determined.

“Let me introduce the Navigator,” Adewara said, motioning for the woman to stand next to him. He pulled Nephrophida's Interactive map from the slate board behind him and split it into two halves, one showing the front side of Aarde, and the other the back side of Aarde.

“I understand we're getting ready to leave but I felt it necessary to reveal information that was only accessible to the Sacred bloodline. The Navigator made me aware of this and I feel it's right that you all know,” Adewara said.

“I read that Navigators couldn't speak,” Abioye said, eyeing the woman. “How did she tell you anything?”

“No, Navigators can't speak,” Adewara confirmed. “They

take a vow to only communicate with their Medjay Guardians and others from their own tribes. They communicate when their bond is formed with their Medjay Gate Guardian after they've given themselves to each other and their love is real. Once the connection is made, they communicate telepathically around the Nabtahenge Gates inside of Khartoum Palace and the Nairohenge Gates outside of Khartoum Palace."

"There are no records of any Navigators of Karnak in the Cheops library records," Aamira said. She had studied Nairohenge lore several years before in the hopes of finding a Gate here but came up empty.

"The Navigator you all see before is from the Dahomey Kingdom located in the Horn of Alkebulan," Adewara explained. "The capital of the Dahomey Kingdom is Ouadane, home of the Ouadane Assassins, and the Dahomey Warriors."

"You didn't answer my question," Abioye interrupted. "How did she communicate all this to you if she can't talk and you are not her mate and Gate Guardian?"

Adewara turned and nodded toward the Navigator. She smiled and began making hand signals, contorting her fingers into different shapes and moving them rapidly. A laugh bellowed from Adewara's chest in response to the movement.

"She says you are impatient and petulant," Adewara chuckled. "I think you'll find her to be insightful. Any other questions?"

Aamira shook her head. Abioye folded his arms.

"Allow me to explain everything," Adewara said. "You'll see that Navigators have at the tops of their elaborate heads; designs woven into their hair that help those who want to use the Nairohenge Gates travel anywhere in Aarde. Think of it like a map. The designs possess the power the ancestors needed to travel.

The Navigators are essential if Sahael is looking to rise once more for the final time. Navigators are accompanied by the Medjay Gate guardians, their protectors and lovers for all eternity."

"So, where is her Medjay guardian?" Abioye asked, looking at the Navigator.

Adewara pinched his lips together and glanced quickly at the woman before focusing again on Abioye. "They were separated after the fall of Sahael. She and her Medjay Gate Guardian were sent away by the Sultan of Horn but were separated after a brief skirmish with the Iceni. Hephaestus, Sultan of Horn, was able to send them through the Nairohenge Gates from M'alqata palace.

"After arriving in the Desert Sand Lands of IFF, the two of them were separated again when the Navigator was picked up and thrown into one of Madame Delphine's cages to be trafficked, after appearing in the middle of the IFFIAN forest during former Queen Adana's skirmish with General Scipio."

Aamira sat forward. "She arrived by portal during the battle with General Scipio? She has been living among us for nine months? Why did she only come forward now?"

"Because she has been searching for her true love," Adewara replied. "And no one knew how to communicate with her. It wasn't until last week when I was giving a public lecture in my official Educator robes that she knew I would be trained in her palm language. Her arrival is a gift from Ishtar and Obatala."

"Why are we here?" Aamira asked quickly. Her patience grew thin. She thought she could sit through another lecture, but every passing moment grated on her.

"First of all, I'd like you both to know more about the Navigators. In particular, this Navigator," Adewara said.

"Understood," Aamira said as she swatted at a fly buzzing around the table. She tried to hide her contempt for being here, but knew she was failing.

"The Navigator and I have spoken," Adewara continued, "and it has come to her attention that there is a knowledge gap with the sacred bloodline that needs to be filled to enhance the Yoruban people. The Navigator feels that the knowledge she shares with you will help you on your way to seeing Sahael rise once again."

"Knowledge gap, as far as what?" Abioye asked.

Adewara pointed to different points on the map before them. "As you know, the Nairohenge Gates were essential to the Ancient Kemites when they were held captive on their home planet of Kolob. Where they disguised Nyathera's asteroid to get away from the Ukáváál. The Ancient Kemites then created space probes that orbited the darkest parts of dark space looking for inhabitable worlds that could house their entire race. Once the space probes found this planet that we call Aarde, they secretly pierced the atmosphere. The probes landed in specific locations, building a single gate in an uninhabited land. The gates, constructed in secret, allowed the Kemites from Kolob to visit Aarde right under the noses of the undead Ukáváál."

"So, the Ancient Kemites didn't all arrive on Nyathera's asteroid?" Abioye asked.

"Yes, and no, but only after Nyathera's asteroid had hit in the center of Alkebulan were the initial gate was built along with the other eighteen that are now located in the center of Khartoum Palace. The Ukáváál however did everything within their power to track and find the Ancient Kemites and were able to use their sentient probes enabling them to travel to different ends of dark space," Adewara said.

"Why is she revealing this to us now?" Abioye questioned.

"As she and I started communicating, it became clear that much of the knowledge of the Navigators has been lost in the past

30 years," Adewara answered. "Even we Educators are not privy to that hidden and sacred information. But now it must be shared or become truly forgotten."

Images of round metal gates flashed in Aamira's memory. She was a child running through a palace with her cousins, passing men and women in silk robes standing in front of a strange shiny ring that almost touched the ceiling and would descend into the floor. Other memories surfaced, though these smelled of smoke in her mind and were tainted by fear.

"I vaguely remember them when I was a little girl," Aamira said quietly. "It's all starting to come back to me. I was being carried on High Queen Nergal's hip running through the center of Khartoum Palace as the Nabtahenge Gates retracted deep into the ground. I remember hearing my mother and the other Queen's talk about how they could be used to save us but the Navigators and the Medjay gate guardians were either killed by the Narsans during the invasion of Sahael or they left through them through the four cities or they fled like cowards. As far as I know, these Guardians and Navigators weren't there when my mother and I needed them the most."

The Navigator made symbols and shapes with her fingers, grabbing Adewara's attention. He nodded and turned to Aamira.

"The Navigator understands why you feel the way you do," he said. "It's justified, but her actions now in helping to lead this people through the tunnels and perhaps even open a gate for us if we find one, will play a significant role in redeeming all Navigators in your eyes."

"What exactly happened isn't all that clear to me," Aamira said. "The Navigators that were killed or died doing their duty. But if others fled like cowards, it was because of them so many died. Their hands are as filthy as Natas and his army."

The Navigator made eye contact with Aamira and continued moving her hands in unintelligible ways.

"The Navigator says they were ordered to leave per King Sekhmet's command," Adewara interpreted. "Your mother, Queen Regent Arishkegal, was there when King Sekhmet gave the order for the Medjay Gate Guardians and Navigators to abandon Sahael."

"Why would he do that?" Aamira said. "Why give such an order? I remember the screams. I remember the smell of burning bodies. If we had used the gates, maybe my parents would still be alive."

"Or maybe all the Navigators would be dead, and the Gates would be useless for the rest of eternity," Adewara replied. "There is more to leadership than merely saving lives. In any case, the fact that you can remember is proof of your bloodline awakening and filling you with the knowledge of your ancestors. This is what Lord Commander Natas wanted to disrupt and sever."

Adewara paused and took a deep breath. "To become a Navigator takes years of training in Timbuktu at the hand of the Educators, Masters, Fellows, Post Docs, Lecturers, and finally the Professors. Prior to that, they are trained as assassins in the Dahomey Kingdom and then sent to Ouadane city to undergo secondary training in the astral realm where it's been replicated in the cities training capital."

"Who do these Navigators answer to?" Abioye asked. "They must answer to someone."

"The Navigators answer to Lord and Lady Talatu, the Sultans of Horn, and are managed by Hephaestus who is known as one of the most handsome black men in all of Alkebulan. Horn is home of the Núcor armored Knights of Horn who are commonly referred to as the N.A.K."

"Where were they when Sahael was invaded?" Aamira asked.

"Horn was dealing with problems of its own during the fall of Sahael. Horn went dark after communication channels were severed and the Nairohenge Gates retracted into the ground. It was protocol to go dark and wait for Sahael to reestablish contact. Had Lord Commander Natas' invasion never taken place, you would have learned about Horn and its dignitaries, and Egyptus's Pharoah's and Ptolemy's. Knowledge you were robbed of by the witans in this world was to keep you ignorant, stupid, and naïve. This is what all witans want, for black people to have no recollection of their past, and history; to manipulate black people in all ways because they fear us and our true potential."

"We overshadow them in every way possible," Abioye said, head bobbing up and down in agreement. "Why else would they want us dispersed from our home?"

"Indeed, you're correct," Adewara said. "However, there are more reasons that will come to light in time as we prepare to leave Karnak."

"How long do we have?" Abioye asked.

Adewara looked at Aamira. "No more than two weeks. That will give Queen Aamira time to recover from giving birth to Yinká. I can tell you're both tired. We can continue talking at a later time. Why don't you head back to the royal chambers and rest."

Grateful, Aamira stood. The Navigator waved her hand to get Aamira's attention.

"What is it now?" Aamira asked, wanting nothing more than to be alone.

Adewara pointed his finger to the Horn of Alkebulan and expanded the area of the map to focus on the region exclusively.

"She wants to tell you more about Horn before you go," Adewara said. "I will interpret if you can give us one more moment. She tells me the King does not need to be here for this if he doesn't wish to stay."

Aamira put her hands on her hips. "Fine. Abioye, would you go check on Yinká, please?"

Abioye paused and looked at the map before shrugging his shoulders. "Sure." He walked down the corridor toward the sweltering summer day without looking back.

"Alright, let us go quickly for the Queen's sake," Adewara urged. The Navigator's hands moved quickly, forming shapes, and shifting right and left at an impressive pace. Adewara nodded and continued speaking. "The Horn of Alkebulan is an area that was closed off to Sahael after the invasion of Khartoum Palace and the four bloodlines were dispersed. The Nabtahenge Gates play a vital role in how Horn is run. The Navigator has informed me that the Iceni, one of the four Kingdoms, is trying to gain control of the Dahomey Kingdom, Nubian Kingdom, and Amazonia Kingdom, is a Kingdom of only women."

"What does this area have to do with the Nairohenge Gates?" Aamira asked.

"When the Nairohenge Gates retracted, Horn itself and the sacred floating island of Horn were all cut off. Nubian guards can't continue to be the protectors of the Emperors and Empresses in the four realms, the four bloodlines in Sahael in Khartoum Palace, and in their respective Kingdoms, lastly Egypt. The Nairohenge Gates make it possible for them to operate and serve Sahael. The Navigator revealed to me that Horn has been left to fend for itself, and I fear Horn and Egypt will be needed if Sahael wants to rise from the ashes once again."

"Horn being left to defend itself can't be all that bad if it's a place as powerful as Sahael," Aamira concluded.

"That's incorrect," Adewara continued. "Horn derives its powers from the Nairohenge Gates, and the power generated from Núkú's engine. However, the Iceni Kingdom, a witan monarchy, has risen to power and is looking to take over the Horn of Alkebulan. Without functioning Nairohenge Gates and the energy they produce, Horn is as weak as any other realm. Having control of the Nairohenge Gates makes Sahael the rightful and true power in Aarde. This will make them the sole superpower if and when Sahael is able to rise from the ashes."

"These Iceni must have had help if they're now a Kingdom on par with the Dahomey, Nubian, and Amazonia Kingdoms," Aamira concluded. She knew only one demon of a man could raise a kingdom to be that powerful in merely a 30-year span. "I'm assuming Natas was involved."

Adewara nodded, running his hand through his dark afro. "The Navigator said these Iceni have come into power with the help of Lord Commander Natas, yes. He has armed the Iceni with the means to fight and experimental battle animals that roam the Horn of Alkebulan, not unlike the oversized creatures once used in Sahael. These Iceni know that the Nairohenge Gates are out of commission and have taken it upon themselves to torment and weaken the other three Kingdoms."

Despite her desire to leave, a familiar wrath trickled through Aamira's veins. All this death and destruction over decades had all been orchestrated by one fallen angel: Natas. Was it even possible to defeat such a being?

"With Lord Commander Natas involved, anything is possible," Aamira said. "When you say, 'experimental battle animals,' what do you mean?"

Adewara looked to the Navigator for her approval to

continue. The Navigator nodded her head in agreement. She grabbed a charcoal pencil and began drawing on a paper with Adewara's scribbled notes. Images of terrifying creatures soon filled the page, many of them tearing people to shreds. The Navigator could have been a successful artist in another life, particularly in the realm of horror.

"Apparently these Iceni have been catching thousands of hyenas, jaguars, tigers, and bears," Adewara continued, eyes fixed on the Navigator's sketching. "They've experimented on them using forbidden and horrendous knowledge given by Natas himself. They infuse the poor animals with Orichalcum and obsidian, morphing bears into monstrous werebears, tigers into beasts twice their size, Jaguars and Hyenas into creatures that cackle and slither. After sending them into the Horn Forest that stretches into all four Kingdoms, the Iceni lost control of the Werebeasts and now they roam the Horn Forest unchecked and unchallenged, invading Amazonia, Nubia, Dahomey, and Iceni itself."

The Navigator finished her drawing and held it up for Aamira to get a better look. The beasts would truly be terrifying in the real world.

Aamira took the page and held it, feeling the rough texture of the weave. "So, without the Nairohenge Gates, the Horn of Alkebulan will eventually be overrun by these Were-creatures, and they will spread all over Alkebulan. That's what you're saying?"

"Correct," Adewara nodded. "The Navigator communicated that the Iceni tried to climb their way up to Horn, but they were stopped by Grootslang, a half elephant python-like creature that's five hundred feet long. Lord Commander Natas and the Iceni decided that it was such an abomination they left it alone to roam Horn Lake. Chaos reigns in the area."

"Serves them right," Aamira spat. She tossed the drawing

onto the stone table. "The Iceni have become the architects of their own demise. Hopefully, they are torn to shreds by their own abominations."

Adewara shook his head. "That won't stop them for long. Natas and the Iceni know that if they can gain access to Horn, they'd have access to Hephaestus's Orichalcum armor."

"Hephaestus's Orichalcum armor?" Aamira asked. "Hephaestus is the Armorer you mentioned that sent the Navigator here, right?"

Adewara looked at the Navigator, who shook her head from side to side.

"That information is for the people of Horn only," Adewara said. "The Navigator won't share it with us. However, as I said before, she has agreed to lead us through the tunnels toward Sahael, stopping first at Nero's Realm for information and a safe refuge. She will stay with the people and blend in amongst the Yoruban until you have need of her assistance from there."

"She's welcome amongst us and will have guards to watch over her in secret," Aamira said.

The Navigator nodded her head and walked out of the library, leaving Aamira and Adewara alone.

"There are many nations waiting for Sahael to rise to prominence once again," Adewara said as they watched the Navigator turn down the long entrance hall. "All of Aarde depends on Sahael for its technology, access to Timbuktu and the four realms for support and protection. It is said the six Sentinel Islands will be united into one when the six bloodlines find their way there together. Whether this is to happen after the redemption of Sahael or before, no one can say. For thirty years slavery and chaos took root in the absence of Sahaelian power. I pray every day for our release from this time of trials."

Aamira stepped forward to leave but turned to face Adewara. "Why did you send Abioye away? He should have been here to hear all of this."

A small smile touched the end of Adewara's mouth. "I have seen the distance you have placed between yourself and your husband since the battle with Scipio last year."

"That distance had begun to grow before that," Aamira defended.

"And I'm not blaming you for it," Adewara conceded. "All I'm doing now is giving you an opportunity to pass along all this information to him yourself. Perhaps talk about other things as well. Consider it an excuse for dialogue."

"I'm in the mood to hold my baby and sleep, not talk," Aamira said. She took a deep inhale and wanted nothing more than to lie down. One question remained in her brain however, and she needed an answer. "What's the Navigator's name? I don't want to call her 'Navigator' forever."

Adewara shrugged. "I don't know her name. She showed me the symbol for it with her palm communication, but I have no way of interpreting it to the common language. Unfortunately, you'll just have to keep calling her 'Navigator' until she is reunited with her true love." He side-glanced at Aamira. "Such romance. It must be wonderful, don't you think?"

Aamira started walking toward the entrance without responding.

She had a bed waiting, and a hungry infant.

CHAPTER III
THE PATH OF MOST RESISTANCE

Nibiru Tunnel, Nambian Sea, Neros's Realm

It took two weeks for the people to prepare for their departure from Karnak. Tens of thousands of Yorubans swarmed the pyramid, each with a specific time designated to enter the Nibiru Tunnel once the royal family, led by the Navigator, had gone through. It would take several days for all the people to travel since the tunnel was only big enough for ten people to walk shoulder-to-shoulder. The halls of Cheops Pyramid were bursting with people as they lined up, awaiting the exodus.

The Navigator stood at the entrance to the Nibiru Tunnel, patiently awaiting her orders. Adewara gathered the royal family before her, arms wide as he spoke. Aamira and Abioye gathered close with their sons. Aamira held Yinká close as the baby pulled on one of her long braids.

"There are multiple tunnels that will lead the people astray if they aren't following the Navigator's path," Adewara warned.

Abioye motioned for General Tantoluwa to step forward.

"General Tantoluwa will lead any stragglers and keep them on the path," Abioye said.

"Thy will be done, my king," Tantoluwa bowed.

"Only a small group of us will travel toward Neros's Realm," Adewara continued. "The Royal family, myself, and fifty members of the Nubian guard. The remaining emerald guard will accompany General Tantoluwa and the people as they find a safe quarter to await our return and thus ensure their safety."

"Good luck," Abioye said as General Tantoluwa entered the Nibiru tunnel and stood beside the Navigator.

"Let's go everyone follow me," Adewara said as they entered the Nibiru tunnel veering off to the southeast.

The green glow of the walls gave light to the group as they traveled. For the first few days, the Navigator led all the people together. Aamira would look back at times, seeing an unending stream of Yorubans stretching the length of the tunnel. She had no idea how far back the group went, but she assumed miles and miles. Since there was no day or night in the tunnel, they would walk until fatigue overpowered them, and the Navigator would call for a halt. Rations of dried fruits and meats would then be eaten, and the population would individually fall into a restless slumber.

Seven days into the trek, the Navigator gave Adewara his instructions, and she split off with the rest of the people at a branch that led north. General Tantoluwa followed her, waving goodbye to the royal family and their guards.

After traveling for several more weeks through the Nibiru tunnels traveling first west, then south, then southeast, and finally due east, Aamira and her kin approached what appeared to be a four-way intersection.

"We are not that far away from Neros's Realm," Adewara said.

"Then why have we stopped?" Aamira asked.

Adewara pointed at the different routes. "We have arrived at a four-way crossing area and need to decide which way we should go. All four entrances will take us East. One leads to the surface of Neros's forest, the others to the southern or northern side of the Neros's realm."

"I thought the Navigator gave you instructions," Abioye said.

"She did, but this part wasn't mentioned," Adewara replied, rubbing his temple. "So far I've just followed the emerald lights, but they're all lit up leading in three different directions."

"So, what do we do?" Aamira asked.

"We send the Nubian guards down the three tunnels and have them report back to us which way we should go," Adewara decided.

"That will take some time, but it's the safe play," Abioye said.

"Indeed, no need to risk any of you or your children," Adewara said.

The Nubian soldiers, all men, divided themselves into three groups of 15 and traveled down the three hallways.

"Now, we wait," Adewara said, sitting down against the tunnel wall and pulling out a pouch of dried grain. He threw a handful into his mouth.

"How long?" Abioye asked.

"As long as it takes," Adewara chewed. "We can set up camp in the meantime and wait for them to return. It could take days for them to go forward and then come back."

They set up their small tent camp with the remaining 15

Nubian guards who acted as their protection. The soldiers created a perimeter of five guards each at the three entrances.

After several hours, the boys grew restless and began playing in the tunnel next to the intersection. As they laughed and chased each other, a scream echoed through the passageway. Aamira jumped to her feet and stared in the direction of the sound. She saw two Nubian guards crawling down one of the side tunnels, dragging themselves by their arms.

"Get the princes out of here now!" one of the Nubian guards ordered.

"What's going on?" Aamira asked.

"Stand back, my queen," the soldier said. "We need to find out what happened."

A group of guards ran up to the injured soldiers and dragged them back to the mouth of the intersection. Both men's legs were bloodied. It was obvious that one of them had lost both limbs below the knees. Their whimpers and cries sent chills up Aamira's spine. Yinká started to cry.

After a flurry of activity that included bandaging up the injured soldiers as best they could, the commanding officer rushed over to Aamira, Abioye, and Adewara.

"The section of the Nibiru tunnels where their battalion was ordered to search was infected by white bioluminescent cockroaches," the Nubian Guard breathed.

"Cockroaches did that?" Yekú asked, pointing at the wounded soldiers.

Adewara stepped forward, gazing down the tunnel as if looking for an imminent attack. "These aren't the cockroaches of Karnak. White bioluminescent hissing cockroaches are the size of dogs with obsidian front pincers, twelve legs, and the ability to fly.

They can spit obsidian ash that can burn through flesh." He turned back to the commanding officer. "What of the rest of the soldiers in that battalion? Are the alive?"

"They weren't sure," the guard answered. "Apparently it was chaos. The roaches used their bioluminescence to hide along the walls in the natural glow. The soldiers didn't know what was happening until it was too late."

"How'd white bioluminescent cockroaches get down here?" Abioye asked, wiping sweat from his upper lip.

"I don't know," Adewara said. "They've been mutated by Orichalcum, so they may be feeding on veins of ore in the ground. We must hurry and head down one of the tunnels that poses no danger."

Aamira shook her head. "No, we need to stay and clean this tunnel out, so these roaches don't hunt down and kill the others on their way to Sahael."

"We don't have the manpower for that," Abioye protested.

"But if we do nothing, the infestation could spread," Aamira countered.

Just as Abioye opened his mouth to respond, a white bioluminescent cockroach flew into the four-way tunnel convergence. Its large body landed in the dirt, wings fluttering and pincers clacking. Pale plates lined its back like an armadillo, but it was larger than any armadillo Aamira had ever seen. The sound of its hiss pierced the ears and sent little Yinká into a fit of screams.

"Run!" Adewara cried.

Yekú, Yemí, and Yomí dodged a blast of obsidian ash fired from the cockroach. The sulfuric gelatin hit one of their tents, which began to disintegrate instantly.

The white roach hissed in Yinká's direction.

"You'll have to go through me, insect!" Aamira shouted as a blade manifested in her left hand.

The Cockroach took to the air as a second soared into view. Abioye leaped at the second cockroach, forming blades in his hand and swiping at the beast.

"Protect Mom and Yinká!" Yomí shouted.

"How do we kill this thing?" Yemí asked.

"Boys, get back," Aamira commanded, but her sons stepped toward the roach without hesitation.

"Keep Yinká safe, Mom," Yekú said, looking over his shoulder. His eyes glowed green. "My brothers! Follow my lead!"

Yemí, and Yomí blinked their eyes, activating their Yoruban gifts.

"We need to figure something out fast," Yemí said telepathically to his three brothers, though Aamira could hear every word.

"I have an idea," Yomí said.

"What're you thinking?" Yekú said.

"Split up and let the cockroach rush Mom and Yinká," Yomí said.

"Are you serious?" Yekú said.

"Yes," Yomí said. *"Then when it rushes forward, Yemí will conjure up Egyptian Glaive Ikakalaka swords and cut the cockroach's wings on both sides, forcing it to the ground. Afterwards, I will manipulate the dirt and residue on its body and create a large spike to impale it."*

"Okay, let's do it," Yemí said.

The brothers did as Yomí said, letting the roach think they were leaving an opening to their mother and the baby, but severing its wings and killing it before it got too close.

"We did it!" Yekú yelled as he jumped up and down.

"What happened over here?" Abioye smiled as he walked up, wiping roach gore from his arm.

"They decided to put me and their little brother in danger by using us as bait," Aamira chuckled.

"How did you know that was our plan?" Yomí asked, shoulders dropping.

"You forget I can hear your telepathy, "Aamira said. "It was a good plan though, and you were able to kill the white bioluminescent hissing cockroach."

"It won't be the last one," Adewara said, running from further up the tunnel. "The guards just killed four more. It's not safe here. I know you want to clear the tunnels my queen, but King Abioye is right. We don't have the manpower. We need to go…now."

Reluctantly, Aamira agreed. They broke camp in record time, killing two more roaches before they started down one of the two remaining tunnels. They continued for hours, long past where they would have rested under other circumstances.

"How do we know this is the right tunnel?" Abioye asked Adewara as they trudged along.

"We don't," the Educator answered. "But there have been no signs of battle, so wherever we come out, I'm going to assume we won't have to fight our way there, which is good enough for now."

Just as they were going to collapse from fatigue, the tunnel sloped upward, and Aamira smelled fresh air. The Royal Family and the Nubian guards walked up to the surface of Neros's forest. It was midday, with sunlight filtering through jungle trees. Humid air swirled around them as birds chirped. Aamira felt the grass under her feet and breathed deeply.

"The tunnel!" Yemí yelled.

Aamira turned around in time to see the Nibiru close like a twisting sphincter.

"Hopefully we're in the right place," Abioye mumbled.

"Where are we?" Aamira asked.

Adewara grinned. "We're in Neros's forest. We need to be headed inward toward his gate for entry into the city of Thebes through Neros's straight."

The seven of them walked through the forest as the Nubian Guards stalked forward in a perimeter formation. Pleasant smells filled Aamira's nostrils. After weeks underground she had forgotten how wonderful the world smelled; how bright the sun could be.

After a few minutes though, something caught her eye hanging in a tree.

It was a dead body, seemingly lynched.

And then there was another…and another.

"Mom, what is that!" Yekú shouted.

Aamira couldn't answer. As she stared into the forest, she saw hundreds of bodies dangling there, all black skinned like her people…like her family. Many of them swung there, eyes open, revealing pale green irises. She held Yinká close to her chest as the baby cooed quietly.

No one spoke as they stood there.

"Something terrible happened here," Adewara whispered.

"What do you think it means?" Abioye questioned.

"This realm has been invaded and destroyed," Adewara

said. "Death hangs everywhere."

"Cut one down," Abioye ordered the Nubian Guards. The men acted quickly, grabbing the closest body, and throwing a hand axe to sever the rope. The corpse flopped to the ground into the grass.

"This land has been marked by Captain Brooks," Adewara said, pointing to a brand burned into the dead man's neck. "Look at the sigil branded into the bodies. It seems Captain Brooks killed as many as he could. They've been here for days by the signs of rigor mortis; perhaps a week. Normally the Ennead would take these bodies back to Naharis's Realm, as we saw in IFF after the battle last year, but for some reason they didn't."

"What did this Captain Brooks come here for?" Aamira asked, as her voice broke.

Adewara shook his head. "Whatever it was, they were here for a reason. We need to find out what that reason was."

"We need to cut these bodies down before they poison the forest," Abioye said. "They're already rotting."

"They deserve a warrior's burial of the highest honor," one of the Nubian guards said.

"Then we do it," Aamira replied. "They deserve nothing less."

After four days of burying the dead, they were finally able to rest. The toil had been exhausting, especially without proper tools, but the job was now done.

Even so, Aamira felt like the dead couldn't rest.

As she sat next to Adewara before a small fire on the fourth night, she could no longer keep her feelings silent. Abioye and the boys were out hunting for the evening meal, so camp was quiet. Yinká lay on a blanket next to her, quietly sucking his toes.

"We've buried them," she began, "but they still are restless. I can feel it in my heart. It's like ever since we heard Nova's song after the battle with Scipio, I can feel the longing of those who pass on."

"I feel the same," Adewara admitted. "The song haunts my dreams. Their souls needed a place to go but could not rest. They needed and wanted to be accepted by Ishtar and Obatala, but their spirits were sent back. They have nowhere to go."

"What will they do?"

Adewara pointed at the Marula trees all around them. "The spirits entered into the Marula Trees, infusing life back into the soil and roots."

Aamira's tattoos glowed as he spoke, as did her bracelet.

"I can feel the truth in your words," she said, staring at the trees.

"Place your hands on the ground," Adewara counseled. "You have a connection with Aarde that will allow you to feel the life around you. Reach out to the spirits and see what you can learn."

Aamira placed her hands on the ground and felt the spirits inside of the Marula Trees re-entering the hanged bodies as if trying to come alive again. Every plant in the forest, every rodent or fox seemed afraid of death to the point of fleeing all life.

"This realm is dying," Aamira whispered. "I can feel the life leaving it. We need to correct it as soon as we can. This needs to be our priority."

"We have many priorities," Adewara said as he stood back up and stretched his back. "Some of them we may be able to do something about. Others we won't be able to. All we can do is our best."

After Abioye and the triplets returned with several birds for dinner, they all slept fitfully in the dying forest. The following day was dark and overcast. Sunlight couldn't pierce the forest.

"Do we know where to go?" Abioye asked Adewara as he threw his pack over his shoulder.

"Without the sun, I'm not sure," Adewara replied. "I had hoped for a bright day so we could find our path."

Aamira looked around. The forest was still. No air currents brushed through the grass. She could hear movement all around.

Her tattoos glowed and she opened her senses to the forest. The eyes of the animals became her eyes. Ancient paths became clear. It took some adjusting, but she soon found a path that led to a circular stone gate embedded in a cliff face covered in vines.

Neros's Gate.

"I've found it," Aamira said. "It's a few miles to the west. Follow me."

The royal family and Nubian Guards walked behind Aamira as she led them through the forest. After an hour they approached Neros's Gate and stood directly in front of it. A large letter 'N' centered in the middle of the large circular barrier. The green symbol of the head of a large bear with its mouth open had been carved near the top. Below the large 'N' were a set of footprints that lit up in their presence.

"Step on the footprints," Adewara suggested. "I believe they are here for you and your bloodline."

Aamira and Abioye did as they were told. The large 'N' lit up. Two sets of handprints appeared with arrows pointing circularly, suggesting that they needed to twist the letter 'N' in a circular motion.

Working together, Aamira and Abioye pushed on the barrier. With all their strength they pressed against the stone until it shifted with a grinding sound. The entire gate lit up and unlocked. A loud click echoed against the cliff face and the door opened. Light poured through the opening for a moment before revealing a small strip of land beyond with water on both sides, as if inside the cliff was a peaceful land hidden from the rest of the world.

A loud roar drew their attention back to the forest behind them. Aamira turned to see white short-faced bears lumbering from the forest. The beasts were massive, reaching six feet tall while still on four legs. There were at least eight of them.

"Mom," Yomí whispered while grabbing her arm.

The bears didn't rush forward or growl, however. They sniffed the air and approached slowly, seeming to bow before the royal family.

"What is this?" Abioye asked, a nervous twinge in his voice. "Should we manifest our weapons?"

"No," Aamira smiled. She reached her hand out to the closest bear and touched its fur softly. The short-faced bears sniffed her and started to lick her face.

"It's okay," Aamira laughed. "They're friendly."

"Amazing," Adewara breathed as the boys began petting the bears and giggling. "These Bears must be part of the Yoruban bloodline. They were called to you, my queen. We now must travel through Neros's Gate, through the small straight fifty-mile section of land before we arrive at the sanctuary.

"We can use the Bears as a means of transportation," Aamira said as the bear nuzzled against her. "They want to take us. I can feel it. They can get us there quickly as we travel through Neros's gates and up the straits."

As if in response to Aamira's words, the bears kneeled before them, allowing them the ability to ride them through the gates.

"What about the guards," Abioye asked, holding tight to the bear's fur. "There are only enough bears for two of them to ride with us."

"Worry not, my king," one of the Nubian commanders replied. "We will make our way on foot. We trust these creatures will protect you. This is the will of Ishtar and Obatala, I am sure."

The royal family passed through Nero's Gate into the pleasant sun of this new world. The air tasted sweet on Aamira's tongue, as did the water of the streams. For hours, the bears ran at speeds that surprised Aamira. Trees blew past them, as did lakes and mountains. The boys seemed thrilled to be riding bears, while little Yinká cried at times, but for the most part slept as the bears jostled them gently.

They traveled for hours until they came to a wall of polished black stone forty feet tall. It towered above them.

"This is the barrier wall," Adewara said. "There should be a gate somewhere that will let us in. It should look like the one that granted us entry to the realm in the first place."

The group turned south and ran along the edge of the wall looking for an entrance. After another half hour of searching, Aamira saw another circular stone gate not unlike the one that had led them to Neros's Realm.

Adewara climbed down from his bear and approached the seal. "The Negrundian Gates. Notice the 'N' symbol here with two

Egyptian glaives forming an 'X.' It means 'Meet eye to eye with your eyes.'"

"Cryptic," Aamira shrugged as she too descended from her bear's back. "I assume we need to do the same thing as before to open the gate?"

"Yes, but turn the letter 'N' in the opposite direction this time," Adewara said.

Again, Aamira and Abioye worked together to twist the symbols. As before, the Negrundian Gates started to open from both sides.

When the gates opened, a rush of air blew through Aamira's braids. Fog billowed and dissipated, revealing a city beyond with tall towers and stone buildings. The royal family stepped through the opening onto cobblestoned ground. The city seemed quiet in the late afternoon sun.

An old man approached quickly, a surprised look on his face. He ran off and after a moment returned with a cadre of soldiers who looked equally surprised to see the visitors. They were dressed in heavy dark matte emerald armor. They all stood six feet eight inches tall, with long wooden staffs tipped with sharp glaives.

A strong man with the same armor as the others, but wearing a red cape, stepped forward. "We are the Negrundian Knights," he shouted. "You are not permitted to enter through the Negrundian halls. State your business and return through the gate from whence you came."

Aamira stepped forward.

"I am the Black Madonna and the last living pureblood of the Yoruban Bloodline of the ancient and sacred heritage," she shouted. "I am the last living remnant of the Yoruban Diaspora, Black Madonna of the sacred six bloodlines and the divine nine bloodlines with equal blood rights as my mother, the Queen Regent of Sahael. You will let me and my family pass."

The Negrundian Gatekeepers fell to both knees immediately, acknowledging the Black Madonna.

"Forgiveness, my queen," the lead knight said, head bowed. "I meant no disrespect. I serve at your pleasure, and the pleasure of the sacred bloodline. The Signs of The Times are upon us!"

"The Signs of The Times are upon us!" the knights repeated in unison, voices echoing along the wall.

"You're welcome to enter Thebes," the knight continued. "Your presence will of course be requested by the stewards of the realm, Steward Ọbalúayé and Stewardess Odùduwà. Their joy will be full, I am certain. I will lead you to them personally."

CHAPTER IV
A REALM OF DEATH AND LIFE

Neros's Realm, City of Thebes

The Negrundian Knights escorted the Royal Family to the city bridge that would allow them entry into the city of Thebes. Aamira looked to the nearby buildings and saw evidence of the earthquakes that continually shook Aarde. Several structures were damaged and cracked, while at least one she could see over the long bridge lay completely in ruin.

"The Negrundian Knights are not permitted entry into the city of Thebes," the lead knight said as they stopped at the bridge. "We are only responsible for guarding and operating our respective halls. We will hand you off to the Thebes city guards. You can see them approaching now dressed in light matt emerald armor and carrying their ceremonial crossbows."

Indeed, the city guard marched across the bridge and stopped before the knights. The guard consisted of men that stood six-feet eight-inches tall and women that stood six-feet five-inches tall. The men all had long dreadlocked hair, and the women had braided hair. The Yoruban Sigil was embroidered on their matte green leather armor. The symbol seemed to glow in the royal family's presence.

Their commanding officer spoke briefly with the knights

before motioning for the Royal family and Adewara to follow them as they were escorted across the mile-long city bridge.

The Royal Family, along with Adewara, were escorted by battalion down the main street of the city of Thebes. Many buildings had crumbled. People hefted stones here and there in a vain attempt to rebuild. Merchants and pedestrians watched curiously as the entourage passed. Children waved to the guards and shouted their names, while a young woman ran up to one of them and kissed him on the cheek before handing him an apple.

They passed a city square surrounded by three-and-four-storied shops, several of which were boarded up due to quake damage. There in the center, Aamira saw a ring of stones in the ground carvings in the rocks.

This was a Nairohenge Gate, retracted into the ground just as the gates had in Sahael over 30 years ago. Aamira stopped to observe them and could see glimmers of blue and green light. There was power here. She could feel it. The Navigator would know what to do, but she was with General Tantoluwa in the tunnels still, far from here.

Citizens of Thebes followed the royal family as the guards continued toward the center of the city. The people seemed to look at these visitors as a sign of hope for things to come.

The guards' course led them directly to a municipal building which they had referred to as Negrunde Hall, a towering white building with walls and floors of ivory stone. Emerald marble inlay gave the stones a greenish hue. Fine woodwork accented the edifice, from the furniture to the molding high above. The place was magnificent and majestic to walk through.

The hall was intact and untouched, as if the quakes had no power to shake these foundations.

The Yoruban Sigil adorned all of the doors in the hall, with small Marula Trees accenting the woodwork wherever Aamira looked.

They finally entered a palace room with tall arching ceilings and a set of thrones sitting on a dais at the top of a small set of stairs.

"You will wait here for Steward Ọbalúayé and Stewardess Odùduwà to address you," the lead guard said as he bowed to Aamira.

Before he could walk away, Aamira grabbed his arm. "We have a contingent of 60 Nubian Guards making their way toward the city now. They should arrive sometime tomorrow. Could you make sure the knights allow them entry and bring them to us? They are our chosen protectors, and worthy of all honor."

"I will pass the message along." The guard bowed again before leading his men out of the palace room.

"This is a nice place," Abioye whispered.

"The city was wrecked," Yemí mumbled.

"I saw a dead body crushed by rocks in one of the destroyed buildings," Yekú added. "There was blood---"

Aamira hushed her family as footsteps echoed behind the dais. Two people as regal as Aamira could imagine walked out, whom she assumed to be Ọbalúayé and Odùduwà, the Steward and Stewardess of Neros's realm.

Stewardess Odùduwà stood seven feet tall with long braided grayish emerald hair and green eyes. She had unblemished and perfect chocolate skin and a slender, muscular frame and well-defined muscles and ivory teeth. Her beauty was stunning, as were her fierce emerald eyes. Steward Ọbalúayé stood seven feet tall as well, with a short, grayish, green-colored afro. His thick chiseled frame invited everyone to take a second look at his towering masculinity. They both wore exquisite clothing that had an emerald embroidered Yoruban sigil within their leather robes.

"Welcome," Steward Ọbalúayé said as he and his wife sat down on their emerald and wooden thrones.

Adewara knelt to one knee. "Steward and Stewardess. I am Adewara, Educator of IFF, leader of the Hashashin Assassins, servant to King and Queen Adesola, whom I present now with their sons, the four crown princes."

Aamira and Abioye knelt as well, as did their children. Baby Yinká laughed and tried to pull away from his mother's arms.

"You all may stand," Stewardess Odùduwà said. "Queen and King Adesola, why have you come to Neros's shores? I would like to know how you were able to navigate through Neros's forest and past our initial gates."

Aamira stepped forward, handing Yinká to Abioye. "I am Queen Aamira Adesola, one of the four black Madonna's of the chosen bloodlines, from the ancient order of the sacred lineage. I have brought the Diaspora from the Desert Sand lands of IFF, unlocking their bloodline through Naki's eternal flame. The Yoruban diaspora are on their way back to their homeland of Sahael."

Empress Odùduwà stood from her throne. "The Signs of the Times are truly upon us! Come, I know you all are tired and weary. You will find rest here. We will talk again in the coming days. Your children are safe and can roam around freely within these walls. They are now under the protection of the Nubian guard, as are you all. They will escort you to dwell in the Sahaelian halls and the estates to the east."

"What about the quakes?" Abioye asked. "We saw a great deal of devastation in Thebes, along with death. Are we truly safe in this realm?"

"Here in the palace and the adjoining estates, you will be safe," Steward Ọbalúayé said, still seated. "The blessing of Nero's Realm extends to these locations. You'll find most of the people residing in these sections of Thebes so they can sleep comfortably at night without fear. We will discuss more in the coming days."

For three weeks Aamira and her family lived in a palatial estate beside a clear stream not far from the Negrunde Hall. During that time, they never saw the Steward or Stewardess even once.

A few days after their arrival, the Nubian Guard were granted entrance to the city and brought to their king and queen. They spoke of strange sights on their journey, seeing spirits in the forest and more dead bodies hanging where the day before there had been none. Aamira didn't know what to think of their tales. Adewara seemed concerned by what they had spoken and spent most of his time studying in Thebe's central library.

Servants saw to their needs during these weeks, and the people treated the royal family as honored guests. Parties were thrown and festivals at least twice a week. During the daylight hours, Aamira and her family would help clear rubble in the city. Thebes seemed sparsely populated for its size, raising the question in Aamira's mind about how many had died in the quakes. The bodies hanging in the forest that they had taken four days to bury continually popped into her mind as well. What had happened here?

The ground shook as often as parties were thrown. While

no buildings had collapsed during their weeks in Thebes, it was only a matter of time.

On a bright morning, Aamira dried herself from her bath when a knock echoed through the house. She threw on her robes and walked to the main entrance hall where Abioye was answering the door. A servant woman bowed to him.

"Steward Ọbalúayé and Stewardess Odùduwà request your presence in the throne room," the servants said. "I am to lead you, if you agree to come."

"We agree," Abioye smiled.

They followed the servant down the estate streets toward Negrunde Hall. Upon entering the palace chamber, Aamira saw the Steward and Stewardess sitting on their thrones just as they had weeks before.

"You may approach," Stewardess Odùduwà said.

Queen Aamira and King Abioye approached Steward Ọbalúayé and Stewardess Odùduwà.

"There are important matters to discuss," Odùduwà said. "I would ask that you listen, and if you understand what it means to be in Neros's Realm?"

"No, what does it mean?" Amira asked.

The Stewardess nodded her head as if that was the answer she expected. "First off, you have set in motion events that cannot be reversed. The reversal of the ocean currents from Western Aarde to the Eastern Aarde have resulted in typhoons, tsunamis, and hurricanes throughout Aarde. That has also resulted in rainstorms causing severe flash flooding on every continent. Now there are Aardian quakes happening everywhere that have started shifting and changing the landscapes, creating untold amounts of destruction. You have seen the results here in Thebes, and I'm sure in IFF before you left.”

“How do we stop it?” Abioye asked.

“Your wife has inadvertently triggered the first gathering,” Stewardess Odùduwà said. “The Signs of the Times will not stop until it’s complete.”

“So, what happens now, since we’ve triggered these events and signs?” Aamira questioned.

“You need to see the consequences of your actions,” Stewardess Odùduwà said, arms motioning wide as if referencing all of Nero’s Realm.

Aamira’s brow creased. “I’m tired of people implying that everything happening in the world is somehow my fault. My ‘actions,’ as you say, have been to try and help our people, not destroy them.”

“And yet they are destroyed nonetheless,” Steward Ọbalúayé.

“And that’s my fault because I was born to a certain bloodline at a certain time?” Aamira asked. “And our people aren’t destroyed. They are here in the realm. They are with our General Tantoluwa safe in the Nubian Tunnels.”

“Not all,” Odùduwà said. “Tens of thousands died after Neros’s Realm was found and Invaded.”

“Is that why the bodies were hanging in the forest?” Aamira asked.

Stewardess Odùduwà blinked several times before speaking again, as if keeping her emotions at bay. “Our Negrundian Knights were wiped out defending Neros’s realm. All the people were killed for no reason.”

“There are people here in Thebes,” Abioye protested, stepping next to his wife.

"One tenth of what once was," Steward Ọbalúayé replied, voice rising in volume. "Captain Brooks invaded with an Armada of militia, somehow able to sail through the Ash water with his armada intact. He ordered his men to destroy most of the people inside this realm and burn Neros's forest down."

"The forest remains," Aamira commented. This entire conversation seemed far too accusatory for her taste, as if she had been the one to destroy the people.

"To prevent the fire from spreading," Stewardess Odùduwà continued. "the remaining Negrundian Knights battled Captain Brooks and his marines. They fought for weeks, weakening Brooks' marines by seventy percent. Your grandparents, the emperor and empress of this realm, were on the verge of delivering a decisive defeat to Captain Brooks until he summoned the Second Commander of The Ennead Legion known to many as Geb. Commander Geb stood seven feet tall, with Obsidian Orichalcum armor matching his Chalcedony ring. He wore a gray cape. He wielded a Benin Ada blade infused with mystical properties that enhanced his combat prowess that also absorbed the souls of those he killed, making his legion more powerful."

Aamira shook her head. "Wait a minute. Go back. You said my grandparents participated in this fight? How is that possible? I thought they were dead. When did this battle take place? We buried the bodies from the forest ourselves the day before we entered Thebes. It couldn't have been more than a week before that."

"Second Commander Geb and 10,000 of his Ennead Legionnaires removed themselves from the bottom of Captain Brook's ship and made their way into Neros's forest." Steward Ọbalúayé spoke as if Aamira hadn't said a word. "Second Commander Geb ordered the second Legion to stand down, and take---"

"Answer my question!" Aamira screamed. Her voice bounced off the tall ceiling and reverberated through the hall as if ordering repeatedly for them to respond.

"The Negrundian Knights were caught off guard by Second Commander Geb and the second Ennead Legion," Odùduwà said, continuing the story. "They were Disposed of quickly, Second Commander Geb took his Benin Ada blade and moved through them like a hot knife through butter, sucking up their souls into his blade."

Aamira turned to Abioye, hands on her hips. "What is going on? This is madness."

"I don't know," Abioye replied as the Stewardess continued her story.

"After a few hours, the Negrundian Knights were wiped out and hung from every Marula Tree in Neros's forest." Stewardess Odùduwà said. "Your grandparents met with Captain Brooks, who forced his way into Neros's Realm killing more people. Second Commander Geb, and the Second Ennead Legion forced their way through the gate entrance. The Second Commander continued killing the Nerosian people until Captain Brook's forced an ultimatum on your grandparents."

"When did this battle take place?" Aamira asked again, stepping toward the Stewards' thrones. "Answer me!"

Stewardess Odùduwà stared forward, words tumbling from her mouth like a voice speaking from the dust. "Captain Brooks wanted Nzingha's Emerald key as a price to stop the slaughter."

"Answer me!"

Abioye grabbed Aamira's arm. "Let them finish. It's like we aren't even here now as far as they're concerned."

"Your grandparents were utterly shocked that Captain

Brooks had heard of Nzingha's Emerald key," Steward Ọbalúayé continued for his wife as if on cue. Your grandparents asked where he had heard and learned about Nzingha's Emerald Key, but Captain Brooks refused to tell them. Your grandparents refused to give up Nzingha's Emerald Key, so Captain Brooks, in his anger, started executing Nerosian men, women, and children. Every one of them. Eventually your grandparents acquiesced, giving Captain Brooks Nzingha's Emerald key in exchange for the lives of the remaining Nerosian."

"Triumphant," Stewardess Odùduwà took over, "Second Commander Geb emerged with Nááthés Onyx Gate Box, another sacred item he should not have possessed. Your grandparents placed Nzingha's Emerald Key in the box. Captain Brooks then made your grandparents emerge through the Nyani's Emerald barrier that protected their bodies, placed them on their knees, and decapitated them both."

Queen Aamira didn't know how to react to what she had just heard. She didn't know her grandparents, so she really didn't feel anything for them, but the story made little sense. The bodies in the forest were fairly fresh, less than a week since death. This battle must have taken place over 50 years ago, maybe more.

Abioye stepped forward as the Stewards fell silent for a moment. He scratched his cheek, eyes focused. "What are the consequences of Nzinga's emerald ancient Kemetic key no longer being in Neros's Realm?"

"What are you doing?" Aamira asked, confused.

Abioye waved his hand as if to silence her.

"Spiritual life energy all over Aarde has started dwindling because of it," Steward Ọbalúayé answered. "Life energy supports life for all Aardians, and the animals and plants as well. The removal of the key, and the deaths of the emperor and empress, set in motion much death. It started with the waters, affecting plant life, animals, and then the Aardians. They'll start dying soon. Odùduwà and I descended from our elements, giving up our godhood, and became stewards of Neros's realm in the stead of the emperor and empress."

"We are using our own life force to sustain Neros's realm and keep the people in this realm alive," Stewardess Odùduwà said. "Nzingha's Emerald key allows Neros's realm the power to protect the Alkebulan people from having their spirits taken before they enter paradise. Nzingha's Emerald key also keeps the spirits within the realms of darkness and other uncontrollable influences not of Aarde from entering our sphere as an ancient evil that is not understandable to anyone."

The palace hall fell quiet. Aamira waited for the Stewards to continue their stilted monologue, but they sat silently, staring forward.

"This is insane," Aamira whispered. She turned again to Abioye. "Why did they answer your question?"

"They're trying to teach something to us," Abioye replied. "I figured if I asked a question that had something to do with what they were saying, maybe they would respond. It seemed to work."

Aamira thought of a question regarding their history lesson, but nothing came to mind. All she wanted to do was leave this strange place. Something wasn't right, and she didn't care to stay and find out what it was.

She turned toward the exit and waved her hand over her shoulder. "We're leaving. You can rule over this crazy place if you want to."

"You both will have to remain here until Yinká's sixteen years old," Stewardess Odùduwà said.

Aamira stopped and turned to face the Stewards. "What did

you just say?"

"Neros's Realm is dying," Stewardess Odùduwà continued. "The Watcher Trials need to be completed by a member of the sacred bloodline. Neros's Realm and the people have six opportunities to get it right. Everyone in your family must be of-age to participate. You cannot leave this realm until it is complete."

"Like hell we do!" Aamira shouted. "And *now* you'll respond to what I'm saying? Are you insane?"

"When your youngest son is sixteen years old, that is when the trials can be attempted per the Nairobi laws," Stewardess Odùduwà said.

"What are you saying?" Aamira asked.

Steward Ọbalúayé looked past Aamira, as if talking to someone taller than her. "Per Realm law, the sacred bloodline must always remain in Neros's realm. You can try to leave if you wish, but the magic of this land will not allow it. Once the Watcher Trials are completed and you retrieve Inkalamu's Heart from Nisine's monument deep in Neros's dark forest, you can leave. We understand this a lot for you to take in and internalize. Take a few days and think it over. We expect a response in four days. You may go."

"I may go?" Aamira asked loudly, muscles as tense as if she were going into battle. "I may go?! Apparently, we can't go anywhere." She stomped toward the Stewards, fists clenched, but Abioye grabbed her and pulled her back.

"Stop, Aamira," he said. "You need to stop."

"Let go of me!" she struggled.

"Aamira!" Abioye shouted. "Stop! We must figure this out. Let's go find Adewara. He will know what to do."

Aamira stopped thrashing and nodded her head. She followed Abioye toward the door, glancing back at the Stewards as she walked. They stared forward, unblinking, unmoving.

What was this place? Were they in hell?

Adewara would know.

He had to know.

"I don't know," Adewara admitted as they sat in the courtyard of Thebe's central library. A pleasant breeze blew through the hedges as birds chirped above in the hazy sunshine."

"What do you mean?" Abioye asked.

"I mean, this realm is beyond my personal understanding," Abioye replied. "I've been paying attention to the animals in particular since we got here last month. They seem to follow some sort of pattern in their movements, like after watching them for a while you know exactly what they're going to do next."

"As if they are repeating a loop," Aamira said.

"Exactly! Except when you interact with them, the pattern changes for a little while before reestablishing itself. It's almost like time is replaying itself over and over again but with slight variations that don't affect the outcome. Remember how the Nubian soldiers said they saw more bodies hanging in the forest as they made their way toward Thebes? We saw no such corpses. Everything on this plain of existence seems to repeat itself, as if one moment in time plays out repeatedly."

"But the people respond to us," Abioye countered. "And

the quakes are random.”

“Again,” Adewara said, shaking his head, “I can’t comprehend how time flows here or how people perceive it. Obviously, our presence sends out temporal ripples that affect things, but how much of an effect that is, I cannot say.”

“You know, this makes sense,” Abioye grinned. “Before one of the parties the week before last, one of the neighbors slaughtered his last cow in celebration, but then yesterday I saw the cow in his pasture again. I was so confused.”

Aamira looked up at a bird perched at the end of a rosebush branch. Was that fowl simply reliving key moments from its existence?

“So that’s why the Stewards wouldn’t answer our questions,” she inferred. “They weren’t similar enough to the questions that were asked the first time they had lived that moment.”

“I think you’re right,” Adewara nodded.

“So, the battle they talked about with Aamira’s grandparents took place decades ago?” Abioye asked.

“It had to have,” Adewara replied. “Probably right before the invasion of Sahael by Natas. All those bodies we buried are probably hanging in the trees again right now.”

The bird flew away. Aamira watched it soar higher and higher until it disappeared.

“Will we get caught in this time loop?” she asked. “I don’t want to find out that a hundred years has passed in the last three weeks because we’ve been living the same moment over and over again.”

Adewara rubbed his beard. “I don’t think so. There’s nothing about any of this in the library here, but I think once the

Stewards took over the realm, their personal energies have kept it alive, but in a state of perpetual renewal. Once Nzingha's Emerald Key is replaced here and members of the Yoruban bloodline are once again Emperors, time's flow will be returned. But as for us, we are not of this realm, so I think time will continue to flow for us as it has."

"So, none of the people around us will age?" Abioye questioned.

"No," Adewara shook his head. "Now, having said all of this, everything the Stewards told you is true. The Watcher Trials are real and must be performed by Yoruban royal blood representatives in six distinct stages. There are only six of you currently in existence, and all of you must be of age to participate. Inkalamu's heart must be taken from Nisine's monument if balance is to be restored here and entrance to Sahael obtained."

Damn it, Aamira thought. She had no desire to live here for 16 years among people simply repeating their lives over and over. What would that life be like for her children? Her triplets would be in their mid-20's by that time. None of their friends here in Nero's Realm would even age with them.

"But we can't leave?" Abioye questioned.

"I haven't tested the boundaries, but I'm going to assume they're telling the truth about the magic seals keeping people inside," Adewara said. "I'll have the Nubian guards run some tests in the coming days, but I'm sure they'll simply confirm my hypothesis."

"What more can you tell me about Inkalamu's heart?" Aamira asked, arms folded in angry resignation.

Adewara smiled, likely sensing Aamira's frustration. "It's sometimes referred to as the heart of Aarde. When ignited it enlivens animals and people who come to depend on its magical power. Neros's realm can no longer distribute Life Energy and the supernatural capabilities that come from the spirits entering Aarde into one of the four bloodlines."

"That's incredible power," Abioye said.

"I'm assuming from what you told me the Stewards said, their life forces are linked to Neros's Realm. Because of it, they can bestow their magical powers on the people because of the sacred blood you share with them. In a way, they're protecting all of Aarde too."

"How selfless," Aamira said, eyes rolling.

"It is," Adewara said, face suddenly stern. "Eventually they will die due to the fact they've used the majority of their life force to sustain Neros's Realm and the people. As a result, they'll need permanent replacements worthy of the Woodstone throne."

Aamira stood, letting the sunshine on her face for a moment. "My priority is to get out of here and find our way to Sahael. Honestly, I understand that I need to do what is best for Neros's Realm and the Nerosian people here. They are my blood, after all. But I don't have to be happy about it."

"What does this mean for the boys?" Abioye asked, still sitting.

"It means they will grow to adulthood in a safe place with good people," Adewara said. "Even with the strangeness of time, this is still a wonderful place. We will live here and act as though one day time will begin to flow normally again, because it will. Go, rest, and then tell the Stewards what you've decided."

A deep breath filled Aamira's lungs. This was a beautiful place of peace and rest, far from the conflicts of Karnak and the political turmoil of Aarde. She could prepare her sons for the Watcher Trials and live happily. She didn't like having the choice taken away from her, but at least this wasn't the colonies or a place where slavery and death waited around every corner.

Could she live here for 16 years?

Whether she could or not was irrelevant.

They couldn't leave either way.

CHAPTER V
THE DEPARTURE

Neros's Realm, City of Thebes

Aamira, Abioye, and the children remained in Neros's Realm for the next 16 years. Their children came of age in Duwisib Palace among people that changed little over time. The four brothers all stood seven feet tall by this time, with chestnut skin, white ivory teeth, and athletic, muscular bodies. They all looked very much alike to Aamira, though they had adopted unique hairstyles all their own. Young Yinká was distinguishable from his brothers by his long thick braids that came down to the end of his neck. Yomí had smaller braids twisted into a singular ponytail that stretched down his back. Yekú had one large braid that went to the center of his back. And lastly, Yemí had braids set up in singlets; large braid chunks corn-rolled down to his back.

Life in Nero's Realm had been a long cycle of repeated events, changing slightly each time with the actions of the royal family, but always returning to a fixed stasis.

Even though the patterns of behavior became apparent over that first few months, Aamira decided it didn't matter. While the people here were stuck in a loop, her family didn't have to be. She and her sons, along with Abioye, Adewara, and the guards that had joined them, helped rebuild Thebes, the gates, and walls. Quakes continued to wreak havoc, but Aamira wouldn't let that stop them. Eventually time would be restored here, and once it was, she wanted to know she had done everything she could to set this people up for success.

Her boys had grown larger and stronger than she could have imagined. The triplets were men now, 26 years old. While living in a realm of peace, she had taught them war, and they would be able to hold their own in any battle she or Adewara could comprehend. They regularly lamented the fact that none of the girls from their childhood had aged during their time here, making romance an impossibility. Yemí in particular longed for a partner and excitedly anticipated when they could leave Nero's Realm in search of a mate.

Baby Yinká was a baby no longer. He would be turning 16 in a few days and was as tall as his older brothers, though not as muscular. He too had begun to feel the pull of time as his peers never changed and always fell back into the same patterns of conduct. His best friend from when he was five years old remained five years old. Yinká had left so many friends behind as he'd matured, he had stopped interacting with kids his age and instead spent most of his time with his brothers.

Adewara had whittled away the years working with the Nubian Guard in the fortifying of buildings in Thebes. He seemed restless, as did many of the soldiers. Life had gone on outside Neros's Realm. Their families would have grown up, perhaps thinking their military sons had died after so many years. Aamira thought often of General Tantoluwa and the Navigator who had taken the rest of the Yoruban people to another part of Aarde where they would wait for the royal family. Were they still alive? Were they still united as a people, or had they fallen into old patterns of distrust and pride?

As for her relationship with Abioye…distance had settled between them like a canyon. They lived together, served their children, but had no physical relationship to speak of.

And they didn't speak of it.

They spoke of nothing beyond the comings and goings of the boys, or the work in Thebes to reconstruct a theater that had collapsed after a quake. Aamira was strangely content with this. She didn't know if she wanted out of the relationship anymore and had no problem simply ignoring it all together.

The day quickly approached in which Aamira and the family would have to leave Neros's Realm. They would all be attempting the Watcher Trials to retrieve the pieces of Inkalamu's heart from Nisine's Monument. Stewardess Odùduwà and Steward Ọbalúayé's life force had dwindled. Time was running out for them and the Nerosian people in Neros's Realm.

Aamira, Abioye, their children, and Adewara were summoned to the steward's quarters the night of Yinká's 16th birthday. Together they made their way to the Stewards' quarters in Duwisib Palace where Stewardess Odùduwà and Steward Ọbalúayé sat on their thrones as always, statues in a timeless dominion.

"Welcome," Stewardess Odùduwà said with a smile. "The time has come, The Negrundian Knights will escort the two of you from Thebes so you may retrieve the Heart of Inkalamu and bring life back to Aarde."

"We understand," Adewara said. "We have been preparing for the last several weeks with supplies. We'll leave under the cover of darkness before the night falls away."

Odùduwà nodded in response and adjusted the bracelets on her arm. "When you return, the Negrundian Knights will be under your guidance and control, and will undoubtedly need direction, leadership, and stability. Your four children will be taken to the north, south, east, and west corners of Nisine's Monument so they can perform their individual trials and retrieve pieces of the Heart. You, Queen Aamira, and you, King Abioye Adesola, will be taken to the Monument gates where you will face terrors fit for the leaders of the Sacred Yoruban Bloodline. You have the responsibility as one of the chosen and ancient bloodlines to restore Neros's Realm and swear fealty to Sahael."

"Your presence in Neros's Realm has made the Sacred bloodline more critical now more than ever," Steward Ọbalúayé said. "Lord Commander Natas is aware of the signs happening throughout Aarde. Once you've saved this realm, you must get to Sahael one way or another. But remember, once we are gone, it falls to you to become Empress and Emperor of Neros's Realm and to rule as your grandparents did."

The name 'Natas' hadn't been spoken by anyone in Neros's Realm in many years. The sound of it was strange in Aamira's ears. She had almost forgotten the wicked fallen demon and the ruin he had brought on Alkebulan and all of Aarde.

"It's been a while since I've heard that name," she said, looking at the tile floor. "The last time I saw Lord Commander Natas was during the fiftieth Royal Rumble when me and my sisters were together before our meeting with Solomon. He had arranged for his wrestler to win the wrestling match, earning the right to procreate with all three of us. I can still see his eyes…" She looked back up and straightened her shoulders. "I know I need to get to Sahael. I just need to figure out a way to do it while ruling Neros's Realm as well."

"That certainly is a logistical problem you will need to solve," Stewardess Odùduwà said as if talking to someone else suddenly. Their patterns in time were beginning to shift to previous moments again. Aamira could always tell how their phrases would suddenly start to make less sense.

"Meanwhile," Steward Ọbalúayé said, "when you return, you'll need to find a way to visit Timbuktu on the island of A.M.I.T. as well."

"How do we even get there without a Nairohenge Gate?" Aamira asked. There is one here in Thebes, but we cannot access it without the proper knowledge and training."

"Timbuktu is where you'll find answers to all of your questions including the history and secrets of the Yoruban people," Stewardess Odùduwà replied, eyes focused once again on Aamira. "Being taught there is considered one of the highest honors. To be educated within the great library Halls of Timbuktu is a blessing. After you've completed the Watcher Trials, you'll have the opportunity to go to Timbuktu if you're wanting to get back to Sahael eventually."

Aamira tried not to roll her eyes. The response had been almost an answer to her question, but that seemed the best she was going to get from these monarchs jumping around through their own timeline.

"It's Imperative that you learn your history," Steward Ọbalúayé said. "There are details and secrets that even Educator Adewara does not know."

"Lord Commander Natas and the witans will do everything in their power to keep Black people in ignorance," Stewardess Odùduwà said. "Now, Yekú, Yemí, Yomí, and Yinká please step forward. Are you prepared to participate in the Watcher Trials with your parents?"

"We are," Yekú spoke for all of them.

"Then the time to depart has arrived," Stewardess Odùduwà stood from her throne, arms out to the world as if in prayer. "As our energies fail, let the Sacred Bloodline triumph in our stead."

"It's time for us to go," Adewara said.

The Royal Family exited the throne room with their guides.

The group exited Neros's Realm the same way they entered 16 years before, traveling south through Neros's forest. Aamira and Abioye blinked their eyes twice, making them Zambian and enabling them to use their abilities to help them navigate as darkness fell. Bodies hung from the trees as if they had been executed yesterday. Aamira remembered cutting them down and burying them over four days, only to later learn of the temporal anomaly of this place and that their work would eventually be undone. The corpses reminded her of the stakes of what they were doing. Death would be around every corner for her and her children.

On the second day, the guides set off with the boys toward the east, since they would approach the monument from the north and needed to hike through the grassy crevasse lands. No guides would continue with Aamira, Abioye and Adewara. They were to be left to the spirits of Ishtar and Obatala to lead them.

Aamira hugged her sons tightly, confident in their skills and artes.

"Be good and do what you're told," Aamira said. "Listen to the guides and follow your instincts."

While continuing south, Aamira, Abioye, and Adewara walked through a marsh that slowed them down. The trees grew strangely here, as if pulled together by their branches.

Adewara pointed at the odd growth as they trudged through muddy water that went up to their knees. "Do you see those Marula Trees built like caves?"

"Why do they grow that way?" Aamira asked.

"Your father tamed them to the Yoruban bloodline," Adewara said.

"How and why? When?" Aamira asked.

"As part of the engagement ceremony, it's the husband's responsibility to find a guardian of the bloodline. Your father ventured into this forest to find the King of the Bears," Adewara explained.

"What types of Bears were they?" Abioye questioned as they continued their sloshing trek.

"You can see for yourself they are heading right to us," Adewara said, motioning his arm toward a group of four big, white short-haired Bears with Zambian colored eyes wandering around the base of the tree. "Just be calm and all will be okay."

The bears stepped into the march and moved toward Aamira, noses sniffing. She quickly pet their coarse fur, feeling a bond with them she couldn't explain. They bowed to Aamira, and she sensed their desire to carry her, Abioye, and Adewara through the dark magical forest.

"They want to carry us," Aamira smiled. "Do you remember the bears that took us to Thebes when we first arrived?"

"Are these the same bears?" Abioye asked.

Aamira shook her head. "No, just of the same spiritual mindset. They are linked to my bloodline. I feel their thoughts. Climb on."

While traveling, they encountered an enormous mountain pass preventing Aamira, Abioye, and Adewara from continuing. The bears wandered over to a small body of water and started drinking. They then stepped into the water with their passengers on their backs.

"What are they doing," Abioye asked as water splashed up to his chest.

"We can swim under the mountain, with the bears," Adewara said. "Hold your breath!"

Aamira sucked in as much oxygen as her lungs could hold and held tight to the bear as it plunged beneath the surface. Icy water swirled around her. Just as her lungs felt like they would burst, the bears erupted from the water.

"I can breathe finally!" Abioye shouted. "I thought I was going to die!"

Aamira looked up at their surroundings and noticed the same mountains looking down on them.

"Wait, we're in the same place," Abioye said, noticing the same thing as Aamira. "Did these stupid bears just swim down and then back up again?"

Adewara climbed off his bear and stepped onto the grass beside the water. "No, they swam forward under the mountain."

"We were just here, Adewara what's going on?" Aamira asked.

"This is a looping river," Adewara said. "Just like the temporal anomalies of the realm, the water is following the same pattern. We'll have to figure something else out."

After an hour of searching the area, Adewara called to Aamira and Abioye. "I found something!" he waved from a rocky outcropping a quarter mile from the water. "Come here!"

Aamira and Abioye climbed over the boulders to where Adewara stood in front of a cave. The bears followed close behind as if they would not leave the Royal couple to face any dangers alone.

"We are in front of a Quadirikiri cave," the Educator said,

smiling. "There's a Yoruban sigil on the wall over here. This must be the way through the mountains. Let's go inside and see where it leads."

With the bears behind them, Adewara led Aamira and Abioye into the dark cavern. Aamira activated her tattoos so they would have at least some light. Something scraped against the walls as several Rock Spiders the size of dogs leaped toward the trespassers.

"Rock Spiders!" Adewara cried. "We need to do something before they catch us in their webs and drain our bodies of blood."

The short-haired bears roared and leaped forward, attacking the Rock Spiders as the royal family and Adewara defended themselves against the shooting webs. Aamira conjured a Yoruban blade and sliced several of the large arachnids in two. More appeared in the glow from her tattoos.

"Go deeper into the Quadirikiri cave," Adewara ordered.

The short-haired bears continued fighting off the spiders, but more swarmed.

"There is an entire hive here!" Aamira shouted.

"Climb on the bears!" Abioye commanded. "We need to outrun them!"

They jumped on their bears and charged forward, stepping on spiders as they plunged into the mountain. After a few minutes, no spiders could be seen in the glow from Aamira's tattoos. Even so, the bears would not stop running. For hours they sprinted, until it became clear they were too exhausted to continue. The bears collapsed, breathing heavily, and curled up to rest.

"We should follow the bears' example," Adewara said as he removed his backpack and began rummaging around for food and water. He pulled out a small crystal and whispered something.

The crystal lit up, giving them light apart from Aamira's glow. "I have no idea what time of day it is, but I'm tired, and I bet the two of you are too. Let's camp here until we are rested."

The short-haired bears situated themselves around their charges, providing protection for Aamira, Abioye, and Adewara.

Wrapped in her blanket, Aamira looked up at the rocks overhead. She enjoyed being underground. It always felt safe to her. A connection existed between her and the rocks of Aarde. They resonated with power that she felt every day, but especially when surrounded by them.

"Are you alright?" Abioye asked, pulling from her contemplation of the cave's comforts. He snuggled close to her.

"I miss our children and hope that they are safe," Aamira said, as her eyes started to get heavy.

"My love, I'm worried about them as well," Abioye replied, scooching even closer. "I hope that they are doing well. You have trained them for this. They will return with their pieces of the Heart, just As we will."

Aamira closed her eyes, feeling the warmth of her husband close to her and not knowing how to respond. It had been some time since they had laid this close.

"I long for a world where Black children can play with others and not be seen as threats due to the color of their skin," she said, voice echoing quietly through the cave. "I long for a world where they can travel without fearing for their lives every second of every day. The only difference is that our children have gifts so they can protect themselves when they need to. The Sahaelians and Alkebulans need protection, and that is why we cannot fail. There are too many black lives that matter and depend on us. All their black lives matter to me."

Abioye breathed next to her, "It has all changed with the

fake narrative that makes people like us be seen as inferior. The witans have been trying to erase our history, making us seem as if we cannot provide for our own people and lacking inadequate knowledge. We need to remember that we outnumber everyone, we're not the less fortunate, and we must change that."

"We will do what we must and get to Sahael to make sure our people are re-educated properly, so they'll remember," Aamira said.

They lay there quietly for a few more minutes. Just as Aamira started to doze, Abioye spoke again.

"Why are you and I so far away from each other?" he asked.

"You're pretty close to me right now," Aamira yawned.

"You know what I mean. We're not…one anymore. We used to be."

Aamira opened her eyes to the darkness, seeing the slight glow from Adewara's stone. Snores echoed from where the Educator lay. She turned and saw the outline of her husband's face.

"I don't know," she answered. "It started a long time ago."

"Can we do anything about it?"

"Do we want to do anything about it? This isn't a new problem, Abioye. You don't seem to want to talk about it, and I feel no need to dredge it up."

"I want to talk about it now. I want to fix it. I want to be with my wife again, smiling and making love like when we were young."

He wanted to fix it. But was he willing to put in the work to make that happen? Was Aamira even willing to put in the work?

"We're not young," Aamira said, rolling back over with a

deep yawn. "If we want to solve this problem, we need to be rested. I'm glad we're talking about it, I truly am, but right now is not the best time to have a deep conversation."

"I understand. Just know, I'm not going to let this go anymore. I love you and want that love to flourish once again."

Aamira fell asleep with those words in her head. He hadn't said them in at least several years. She hadn't either. Could they fix things? Had too much time passed? She couldn't answer those questions now in this cave, but she hoped the eventual answer was 'yes.'

Abioye gave Aamira her space the next day but remained close to her as they rode the bears through the cave. After eight hours of travel, they came upon the exit of the small Quadirikiri Cave. Light shone as a pinprick far ahead, bringing a smile to Aamira's face.

As they approached the exit though, the ground and walls seemed to move and scamper about. Hundreds of bright red eyes glowed before them.

"Damn it," Adewara breathed. "More Rock Spiders!"

They were the size of cats with twelve legs. Their oval-shaped bodies were covered in eyes above their thick hair. The spiders dragged their bellies on the ground with sharp spikes on their abdomen.

Aamira leaped from her bear, forming green blades in her hands before she hit the ground. She rushed the swarm, slicing haphazardly as warm spider blood speckled her body. Adewara and Abioye joined the fray as well. The bears roared and slashed at the arachnids. Within minutes, hundreds of spiders lay dead, but thousands more spilled from cracks ahead of them, cutting off their escape.

Soon, the cave spiders surrounded Aamira, Abioye, and Adewara. The bears had retreated farther into the cave and whimpered.

Aamira looked around for solutions. Specks of dirt fell from the ceiling, hitting the spiders' eyes. They would respond angrily and scratch at the bits of debris.

"The eyes of these spiders are sensitive," Aamira said.

She noticed up above multiple webs covered in dust that had not been disturbed in some time.

"Be prepared to run," Aamira said.

Closing her eyes, Aamira felt the rocks and dirt all around her. The ground shook slightly. The spiders paused their advance as the quake continued. Dust fell from the ceilings. Irritated, the spiders tried to rub the dust away, but as more fell, they balled up to keep from having their eyes affected, making them vulnerable and at a disadvantage.

"Kill them!" Aamira shouted.

With surgical precision, Aamira, Abioye, and Adewara sliced through the spiders in an incredible display of execution.

However, another set of spiders emerged, awakened by the quake, a hive of flying spider wasps the size of eagles.

Aamira conjured glaive spears and chucked them at the swarming arachnids, forcing them to fly deeper into the cave.

"Run!" Adewara cried. "Run now!"

They charged into the sunlight, followed by the bears.

Standing on a cliff overlooking a jungle valley below, Aamira breathed deeply of the fresh air. No spiders crawled or flew from the mouth of the cave. They were safe.

"What's that in the distance?' Abioye asked while catching his breath.

Aamira looked toward the lush valley, seeing a shining pillar of emerald stone reaching high in the sky directly in the center of the valley. It had to have been well over a quarter of a mile high, with a base of at least a thousand feet. Even at this distance she knew she had never seen anything like this before.

"It's Nisine's monument," Adewara said. He pointed to the far end of the valley, at least twenty miles away. "That is where your sons will be approaching the monument from, on the north."

"I've never seen anything so tall and huge," Abioye said. "How was it built?"

"By the hands of our ancestors," Adewara grinned. "It is a testament to what our people can create when united under the power of Ishtar and Obatala."

It took several hours to climb down from the cliff into the humid jungle. Water dripped from large leaves and rivers flowed all around. Aamira refilled her empty water skin and picked berries and mushrooms to add to what remained of her rations. They camped for the night and started a fire to cook a wild pig Abioye killed. The insects made sleep difficult, but by morning, Aamira felt refreshed and ready for the trials.

Six hours later, they arrived at the base of the monument. It was every bit as tall and even broader than Aamira had guessed from the high cliff face. The obelisk they had seen sat on a large stone complex building at least a half mile long on each of its four sides. Aamira felt like an ant next to the imposing structure.

"You both will have to use your Artes to make yourselves

indestructible," Adewara said as he touched the smooth green stone. "A sacred power is confined within the Yoruban bloodline that needs to be unlocked. We need to find the southern entrance."

"I see a character carved in the rock over there on the obelisk, but no door," Abioye said, pointing at the symbol of two eyes surrounded by intricate flourishes. As they approached, the symbol began to glow green.

"What is this?" Aamira asked as she observed the carving.

"The eyes of NeRu," Adewara replied. "One was Andalusian, and the other was an ancient Kemite. Each gave one of their eyes to ensure that all Alkebulans and Sahaelians throughout Aarde could be looked upon and watched over at all times. They each donated one of their eyes to Sahael, who created the eye of NeRu that allowed the royal families the ability to see all over Aarde. NeRu's eyes, unfortunately, never had the chance to activate. It was rumored that during the Katunkumean war that NeRu was killed by Lord Commander Natas or locked away to prevent Ishtar and Obatala from finding them."

"How do we get inside of Nisine's monument?" Aamira asked as she studied the image on the monument.

Adewara stepped back. "If it works like other monuments of this type, try standing in front of the eyes. They should interact with yours. As this happens, your eyes will then trigger an opening, allowing us to enter Nisine's Monument."

Aamira and Abioye stepped in front of the eyes. As they did, their tattoos lit up, interacting with the NeRu's eye. Emerald dust poured from the image like a sentient mist, swirling around them with no need for wind or air currents. The mist coalesced in front of them and transformed into a personage of a tall, beautiful black female with Zambian colored eyes, hair, and well-built frame. She stood before them transparent as a ghost, a voice from the ancient past.

"Welcome," the spirit said, voice strong and resonant. "You of the royal Yoruban bloodline are permitted to enter and attempt the Watcher Trials, after proving your true lineage. I am Nisine, for whom this monument testifies. Tell me, have you come for the trials or some other purpose?"

"We have come to attempt the Watcher Trials," Aamira said. "I am Queen Aamira Adesola, and this is my husband, Abioye Adesola."

"Only the pure blood from the Sacred Bloodline is allowed access to the Watcher Trials, and it must be proven by blood," Nisine said, conjuring a dagger and handing it to Aamira. "Cut your finger and cover NeRu's eyes in your blood."

Aamira pricked her fingers, placing her blood on NeRu's eyes. The entrance dissipated into Emerald and opened a door into the monument's dark interior.

Let's go," Abioye said, stepping forward.

"Hold," the spirit said, hand raised. "To retrieve what you seek, six must enter separately. Six must complete the trials alone and unaided. Four others entered this monument two days ago---"

"The boys!" Abioye said excitedly.

"Only one of you may enter here," Nisine continued. "The sixth must find the final path and follow their destiny to victory or madness. Only a pureblood can enter here, and that pureblood is Aamira Adesola, Queen as prophesied."

Abioye nodded his head and started looking up and down the complex walls for another access point. "Go, Aamira. We'll find another way in." Abioye hugged and kissed Aamira quickly. "I will not fail you or our sons. I promise."

Nodding, Aamira smiled. "I never doubted that for a

second."

Adewara stepped forward and placed something jagged in Aamira's hand. "Here. Take my glowing stone for light."

"No," Aamira said. "Give it to Abioye when he enters. As a pure-blooded queen of Sahael, the light from my blades has always shined brighter than his. Let him take it.

"Yes, my queen."

"You may enter," Nisine said.

Aamira stepped through the doorway into darkness, praying her boys were safe, that her estranged husband would survive, and that she would live up to the prophecies of her ancestors.

CHAPTER VI
NISINE'S MONUMENT

Neros's Forest, Nisine's monument

Once inside, Aamira formed Glaives in her hands to give light to the area. Rubble covered the ground as if the ceiling had collapsed at some time in the past. She looked up into the darkness and couldn't even see the ceiling. The air was still and quiet. Her skin tingled. For a moment, Aamira wasn't sure she was even in Aarde anymore. Had she been transported to a different realm, not unlike Nero's where time and space followed different sets of rules?

It didn't matter. She needed to pass the trials and hope her family did the same so they could reunite the shards of Inkalamu's Heart and heal Neros's Realm before traveling to Sahael.

Aamira traveled deep into Nisine's monument and made her way past the rubble, dirt, and dried bones that littered the ground. After several hours of walking, she knew for sure she was not merely inside the monument. This endless space was something else entirely than simply the interior to a large building. She entered a great hall with pillars all around. The darkness went on forever outside her glowing blades and tattoos.

Narrow halls branched off on all four sides. Above the entrance to each hall were symbols of all four sigils from the four bloodlines that represented Sahael. Aamira recognized that they were the same symbols she had seen in Karnak.

She chose the hallway with the Yoruban symbol of a giant Bear face with its emerald eyes and mouth wide open. Aamira walked further down the hallway and noticed a second sigil; it was the Orishan symbol of a giant water dragon's face with its cerulean eyes and its mouth open wide. Next to Orishan sigil, a pedigree chart was etched into the wall tracking her cousin Oadira's lineage.

Aamira got more than halfway down the hallway and saw the Hausan sigil of a large griffin face with its diamond-colored eyes, mouth agape as the others. Like with the Orishan symbol, a pedigree chart tracked Heziara's lineage on the wall next to it.

Now Aamira understood the pattern. Farther down the hall, the Demirrian sigil of a White Rhino with its magical horn and Candelarian eyes was etched beside a pedigree chart that tracked Damisiah's lineage.

What does this mean? She asked herself.

Aamira exited the long hallway into a rounded chamber with marble floors. Darkness continued to reign everywhere outside the confines of her glowing weapons. Here in the space Aamira noticed the Lysinnian and the Rysallian sigils and bloodlines on opposing walls. Large sections of text accompanied the signs and family trees.

Aamira started to read.

The four ancient bloodlines, according to this pedigree chart, a part of the chosen bloodlines, broken down into the sacred, divine, and cursed ancestries. The Rysallians are not part of the Chosen bloodlines.

Aamira glanced at the Lysinnian sigil. It was the first time

Aamira had seen it. The face of a Yoruban martial arts master with its face covered and double-chained Kama sickles stared back at her. The Yoruban Master had Sillimanian eyes.

The pedigree chart looked the same as all the others, until Aamira saw the last name in the line: Adewara. The Educator was of the Lysinnian bloodline.

Next to the Rysallian symbol of a lion's head with its mouth opened and Hazel brown eyes, Aamira expected to see the final family tree carved into the walls, but there was no chart to be found.

"These are the six sacred bloodlines that were sent down to Aarde nearly five hundred years ago," Aamira said quietly, voice echoing through the darkness.

Aamira approached the center of the room, where a spiral staircase of stone led downward, deeper into the ground of Aarde. She descended the stairs quickly, emerging into a short hallway ending with a black obsidian door. The stone shimmered against the green light of her glowing swords. The image of a Marula Tree filled the door's center. Aamira touched it and the door slid open with a grinding sound.

Crickets suddenly could be heard in the silence, as if Aamira had stepped outside into a moonless night. Large Marula tree stumps filled the space, covered in mist. Aamira looked up to see if any stars blinked down on her, but nothing but blackness stared back. The area was mysterious, dark, and moist against her feet, like a marshland had manifested inside the monument. Wandering spiders the size of large cats jumping from stump to stump as Aamira slowly made her way forward. Like the rest of the monument, this strange area was pitch black beyond Aamira's glow.

Quickly the marsh grew deeper, coming up to Aamira's

waist. She began to understand why the spiders were jumping on the stumps. She climbed from the cold grime onto one of the Marula stumps and began jumping from one to the next.

This continued for the next little while as Aamira leaped and stumbled but avoided falling into the dark mud. At one point during a jump, Aamira looked up and could see the stone ceiling above for the first time. She was indeed still inside. What truly caught her eye though were the bird-sized wolf-like spiders casting shadows on the marble ceiling as they crawled around. They were above her in the dark at all times.

She stopped and pointed her Glaive upward for a better look. Greyish brown agile hunters scampered around on the ceiling, with the few she could see in the light seemingly following her.

Hunting her.

Aamira tried to keep her breathing calm and under control. If they attacked, she would be at a disadvantage with no solid ground around here beyond the collection of stumps. Aamira looked to the next stump, sweating profusely.

As she jumped, a spider dropped onto the stump she had been aiming for. With expert speed, she sliced with her blade, killing the arachnid. The action put her off balance however, and she fell into the cold, muddy water with a loud splash.

Aamira scrambled to climb back on the nearest stump, but spiders descended on thick webs all around her.

Soundlessly, Aamira jumped onto the stump and attacked the closest spiders aggressively. She sliced at their webs, making them fall into the swamp, while severing their legs and heads with every strike.

But more spiders descended.

Knowing she couldn't remain still, Aamira leaped to the next stump, and the next, as fast as she could, hitting spiders while soaring through the air. The creature clawed at her as she cut them down, splitting them in two.

Eventually, Aamira's path cleared. She jumped from stump to stump as quickly as she could. Up ahead, her light glowed on what looked like the entrance to another set of trials. It wasn't the walls that best first reflected the light though; it was the massive spider web blocking the entrance. There in the center was a Wolf Spider as large as a horse hissing and waiting for its prey.

Instantly Aamira knew fighting the creature alone would be suicide. Speed had to be her ally. She jumped from the last stump into the dirt and stone less than twenty feet from the entrance.

She ran. She ran faster than she had in her life.

The spider dropped from the web, pincers clicking in the quiet dark. Aamira threw one of her glowing swords just above the spider's head, causing it to rear up as if under attack. Aamira dove under the beast, sliding in the dirt and jumping back to her feet behind the spider.

Aamira didn't stop running. She plunged headfirst into the darkness with only one Glaive to light the way. No walls seemed to be around her. After a few minutes, her footsteps sunk into the sand, making running difficult.

Catching her breath, Aamira saw that she indeed stood on sand. As she reached down to touch the granules, a blazing light suddenly shone from above, every bit as bright as the sun. Heat became stifling in an instant. The glowing Glaives in her hands dissipated as their light was no longer needed.

Now able to see clearly, Aamira looked over a barren sand desert that stretched as far as her eyes could see. No sun shone above, merely a mist that glowed brightly, hanging along what

Aamira assumed to be the ceiling, though she couldn't see it.

Patches of sand shifted around her, revealing the dens of more spiders, bigger than the ones from the hallway. Several popped from their hiding places, revealing six-eyed sand spiders the size of alligators with eight-foot-long legs. They were a brownish sandy red color that was noticeable when they weren't hiding beneath the sand.

Everywhere she looked, Aamira saw shifts in the sand as the spiders beneath became restless.

"How do I get across?" Aamira asked herself as she looked over the large desert.

The stifling air made Aamira sweat, and with no shade to speak of, she knew she couldn't stay exposed for long. She would go through what little water remained in her water sack too quickly unless she pressed forward.

Only one option seemed viable.

She started to run.

Soft sand amplified the effort needed to put one foot in front of the other. As she charged forward, she began to breathe heavily in the sweltering heat. Each step seemed to trigger an angry spider to claw out of the dunes. After a few minutes, Aamira looked behind her to see a dozen terrifying spiders on their long thin legs, scrambling after her.

She ran harder. Still more spiders scurrying from the sand at her intrusion into their sanctuary.

Still, she would not give up. She would not slow down.

Her lungs screamed at her to stop running. Her legs felt like they would collapse beneath her, but she ran on.

Just as she felt like she would pass out from exertion, the sand beneath Aamira suddenly shifted and swirled into a whirlpool of tiny granules. She sank to her waist and tried to claw at the sand to pull herself out, but nothing solid existed beneath the twisting desert. She coughed on the particles now filling the air. Glaives formed in her hands, and she stabbed them into the sand, but nothing worked to slow her descent. The whirlpool swiftly sucked her toward the sinking center in a roar of tiny granules scraping against each other.

Taking a deep breath, Aamira was pulled beneath the surface into darkness.

Instead of being buried until she suffocated, Aamira suddenly dropped as if the ground fell out from under her. She landed on hard stone as sand tumbled all around her.

"Where am I now?" Aamira asked softly as several coughs wracked her chest. Her entire body ached, and Aamira wanted nothing more than to lie down and go to sleep.

No light could be seen anywhere. She smelled vinegar in the air.

Manifesting her green Glaives once again, a pale glow illuminated the area directly around her. Highly polished stones made up the floor at her feet.

Lightning stuck out of nowhere, lighting up the area for a second before thunder boomed in the distance. More lightning followed, showing that Aamira stood on a platform a hundred feet above a dark forest. A mile in front of her stood a large obelisk.

She felt in her heart that this was the end of her trial. Getting to that pilon would take every bit of strength and endurance she had left, which wasn't much.

Stepping to the edge of the platform as lightning continued to strike in the distance, Aamira saw thick strands of almost clear white thread stretching all the way to the ground in rectangular patterns.

Just like a spider's web.

A big spider.

In that moment, she knew the only way down would be by using the web, which would alert whatever gigantic arachnid had built this web. From there, she would need to run to the obelisk at top speed.

She wasn't sure she could do either of those things. Her legs burned and her body cried out for rest.

Now was not the time for self-pity or a defeatist mindset though.

Before she could talk herself out of it, Aamira leaped down toward one of the wire-like spider webs and grabbed hold, sliding down at terminal velocity. Wind blew through her braids as the ground approached.

Without warning, the web bounced violently, forcing Aamira to lose her grip and fall the last twenty feet to the jungle floor. She rolled forward on impact to minimize the damage the fall would do to her knees and ankles.

Aamira shot to her feet and looked back up toward the platform above. A blast of lightning accented the outline of a giant spider unlike anything Aamira had ever seen. The creature had to be 20 feet tall, with more legs than she could count; she estimated 26. The beast had a red-orange cephalothorax and a black abdomen with yellow rings outlining rows of red spots. Two minor red marks accented its belly. The web vibrated as the massive spider crawled down toward its prey.

Aamira sprinted away, blinking her eyes, and activating the emerald protective shell that would help keep her invulnerable. It was a hard Arte to maintain, especially in a battle situation where concentration could be easily broken, but it was a better plan than trying to cut through the hide of that otherworldly monster.

More webs littered the forest, connecting the trees and covering sections of ground. Movement in her periphery informed Aamira that smaller spiders were taking notice of her movements. She looked over her shoulder as she ran but saw no other arachnids in pursuit. It was as if they were as afraid as she was.

The sound of tree limbs breaking and trunks shattering followed close behind her as the giant spider crashed through the sanded wooded land.

Aamira's eyesight seemed tinted with red and ragged gasps wracked her chest.

She only needed to run a little more.

Just a little more.

Her body was tired of running. Part of her wanted to turn and face her fight while fighting to her death. It was a natural instinct, but one she knew wasn't smart. She hadn't come here to die in her pride, but rather to save innocent people enslaved and suffering.

She would run for them, not for herself.

The thought gave her strength as she jumped over a fallen log and saw the obelisk through the trees.

Just as she reached the obsidian structure towering into the darkness, The spider smashed through the trees and reared up in front of her, slamming its front legs into the stone structure. A deafening hiss emanated from the creature. Its pincers dripped with venom as it tried to nudge closer to Aamira as she pressed her back against the obelisk, unable to move in one direction or the other.

The walls behind her glowed green suddenly, forming the shape of three circles. Aamira's bracelet and two rings she had worn her entire life also lit up.

"I need to place the rings and my bracelet on the three

circles on Nasik's obelisk," Aamira breathed as a spider leg swung at her, forcing her to duck.

Desperate, Aamira turned and pulled off her rings. As she touched them to the circles, it was as if the rings were pulled in by magnets. She did the same with her bracelet, feeling spider venom splatter against her shoulder. It didn't matter. She couldn't turn to defend herself. She needed to solve this problem and deal with the consequences if it ended up being the wrong choice.

An emerald mist billowed from the obelisk and surrounded Aamira. She looked back at the spider. The beast dropped its legs from the pilon and stepped back, seeming almost calm. The spider suddenly turned and faced the forest, as if acting as a guard.

"What is going on?" Aamira breathed. She leaned back against the pilon and collapsed to the ground, no longer able to keep her legs under her.

The green mist swirled in front of her and formed the ghostly image of Nisine, the beautiful and powerful queen of old.

"Aamira of Sahael," the spirit said loudly, "Queen Adesola of IFF, daughter of Queen Regent Arishkegal. You have completed the three watcher trials, showing that you two will be the ones to replace Steward Ọbalúayé and Stewardess Odùduwà."

Aamira tried to stand, but found her body would not respond to her brain's commands.

"There is no need to exert yourself anymore today," Nisine said with a smile. "You have proven your humility and fortitude. Instead of fighting battles you could not win merely to satisfy your pride, you ran forward with the thought of the welfare of others in your mind. You will be blessed for this focus and warmth."

"My…sons…" Aamira said as breaths continued to suck in and out of her exhausted chest.

"You will see them soon. They are worthy of your efforts, as is your husband, King Adesola. Rest now and awaken in safety."

If Nisine spoke any more words, Aamira did not hear them. Her eyes closed involuntarily, and she entered an oblivion only someone who has truly given everything they can, will ever know.

Aamira opened her eyes to a new and foreign place. The sun was warm on her skin and the grass on which she lay was surprisingly soft, smelling freshly sweet. A large palace loomed in the distance several miles away under a deep blue sky. Aamira felt refreshed and whole, as if she had slept for a week and eaten a meal fit for a king.

"What is this place?" Aamira asked in amazement as she stood up in a lush meadow of flowers that stretched to the horizon. "Am I dead?" she asked the slight breeze.

"You are not dead," a woman's voice chuckled. Aamira turned to see Nisine's spirit form again, floating above the swaying grass. "You're in the Astral realm, the home of the Watchers, Stewards, and the Gods. The ancient power of Nbata playa runs through every gate in Aarde created by the ancient Kemites. I sent you through a Nairo Gate to rest here. These gates grant the ability to travel directly to Katunkumene. As a compromise, the old gods made the astral realm for those with the ancient blood of the Kemites. To unlock the power of Nbata playa, so that the ancient and the solar bloodlines can return to Sahael and Alkebulan. Once the first and second gatherings have commenced, Alkebulan will be whole."

"What do I do from here?" Aamira asked.

"We are not ones to give knowledge when you can discover it for yourself," Nisine grinned. Her spirit faded away, leaving Aamira alone in the meadow.

"Somehow I knew you were going to say that," Aamira shrugged. She turned and started walking toward the majestic palace in the distance.

CHAPTER VII
THE ASTRAL PLANE

The Astral Plane, Nisine's Palace

"This palace is beautiful," Aamira said as she stood outside the palace gates. Nubian guards consisting of a man and a woman stood at attention. The man was seven feet tall and bald, while the Nubian woman was six feet five inches tall with short black hair. They both possessed gorgeous dark skin, white Ivory teeth, long legs, and well-defined muscles.

The Nubian guards didn't say a word to Aamira as she approached, nor did they open the gate.

Aamira stood there for a few minutes expecting something to happen, but the wind blowing around her was the only movement she noticed.

Horns suddenly blew from beyond the gate. What appeared to be a royal delegation consisting of multiple guards marched down the cobblestone street toward the palace entrance. As they drew closer, the gates opened and the legion of soldiers parted, revealing two people riding large saber-toothed beasts that Aamira had read about in her books. They were called Bunyip's and considered to be mythical. The people on their backs were obviously important, wearing ancient Egyptian clothing and holding hands. Golden Nemes headdresses sat like crowns on their heads.

The Bunyips rode forward, slobbering on the cobblestones, and stopping a few feet from Aamira. A guard stepped forward, chest out.

"To all who would enter," the man cried, "I present Oxossi and his wife, Sariah! Sariah is a part of the lost Nibiru and Ouadane bloodline scattered and dispersed all over Aarde."

The royal couple dismounted their Bunyips. Sariah stood six-feet-five inches tall; she had long braided hair, caramel skin, long muscular legs, and a slender frame. Sariah also had Zambian colored eyes that matched Aamira's.

Oxossi stood seven feet tall. He had gray dreadlocked hair and a well-trimmed beard. Oxossi possessed a chiseled, muscular frame and white ivory teeth.

"Welcome," Sariah said with a slight nod of her head.

Aamira knelt before them as a sign of respect.

"There is no need for you to kneel," Sariah smiled. "Black people don't kneel in the Astral plane. We show respect by nodding our heads to deities of their bloodlines. You've completed the Watcher Trials, relying on your Yoruban Gifts and nothing but your wits. You've done what no one was able to do. Many have tried, and many have died, but only a Black Madonna could've completed such a difficult and daunting task."

"What about my family," Aamira asked, standing back up. "My husband and sons entered the monument from different sides. We were told six people needed to complete the trials."

"And you are correct," Oxossi nodded. "But they could not complete their tasks until you completed yours as the matriarch of the Yoruban line. I have no doubt they will be successful and join us here in time. You did well, daughter of Sahael.”

“Thank you for your kind words,” Aamira said, happy to hear her sons were still alive.

Sariah looked to the sky as if listening to someone speak. “Nisine has informed me that your sons and husband have all individually succeeded in their trials. You have an impressive family. I will bring them here to join you now if that’s what you wish.”

“It is Indeed,” Aamira grinned.

Nisine’s emerald mist appeared, forming into one of Nebuchadnezzar’s Emerald portals. Abioye stumbled through, falling into Aamira’s arms. He was bloodied and bruised.

“Abioye,” Aamira cried.

Her husband smiled weakly. “I did it…” he breathed. “I did it for…you.”

The boys stepped through the portal as well, each obviously exhausted and beaten down.

“Worry not,” Sariah said as the family embraced. “All of you will have time to rest and recover here in our realm. You will feel peace and healing to your souls.”

Finally, Adewara stepped through the portal, confused, and elated to see the royal family.

“You’re alright!” Adewara shouted as he hugged Aamira. “It’s been several days, and I hadn’t heard from any of you. I had become so worried.”

“We’re okay,” Aamira laughed. Tears came to her eyes as she embraced her sons again.

“Why have you come to the astral realm?” Sariah asked.

"We have come to help save Neros's realm and all aspects of life that live on the continents of Aarde," Aamira replied with sadness in her voice.

"What has happened to put Neros's Realm in a dubious position?" Sariah asked.

Aamira turned around to address Sariah. "Captain Brooks and the second Ennead Legion commander Geb have invaded Neros's realm, killing men, women, and children. They destroyed each of the five halls and the city of Thebes. We have spent the last 16 years helping to rebuild, but the Stewards' life forces will no longer sustain the realm."

"What did Emperor Adisa and Empress Adia do to save the Nerosian people?" Oxossi asked.

Aamira experienced a wide range of emotions in that moment. "You speak of my grandparents. They are both dead. We have been sent here by Stewards Ọbalúayé and Odùduwà to complete the watcher trials. Captain Brooks forced my grandparents to emerge from Kyani's emerald barrier into Thebes city. Emperor Adisa and Empress Adia did not want to risk more bloodshed. For this reason, they gave up Nzingha's Emerald key."

"So, your grandparents gave up Nzingha's Emerald key, to save the Neros's Realm," Sariah nodded.

"After Captain Brooks gained possession of Nzinga's Emerald key," Aamira continued, "Second Commander Geb of the Ennead Legion took Nzingha's Emerald key, placing it in Nááthés obsidian box. Afterwards Second Commander Geb quickly took the Ennead Legion back to Captain Brook's ship. In all his anger, Captain Brooks killed my grandparents and many more Nerosian's as he left Neros's realm for good."

Adewara walked up slowly to Sariah and Oxossi; he bowed his head gently. "Without Nzingha's Emerald key in Neros's

Realm, the spiritual power of Life Energy that enters the Sahaelians and Alkebulans people, providing them the light of Katunkumene, will be lost forever. The ramifications of Nzingha's Emerald key will have a devastating effect on all animals, preventing them from reproducing, killing them in the long run. There can be no entry through Neolithic's gate and chamber to access the power in Neros's realm."

Sariah and Oxossi's eyebrows lifted while listening to Adewara speak.

"Do you understand the significance of Nzingha's Emerald key no longer being in Neros's realm?" Sariah asked. "Nzingha's Emerald key unlocks Nabopollassar's four seals fixed on Nullify's gate in Naharis's realm. Aamira, your mother, Queen Regent Arishkegal, and your father, King Regent Enqi, helped put the Emerald seal on Nullify's Gate. The other Queens and Kings of Sahael had Solomon do the same in the other three realms. Solomon, the protector of Aarde, assisted the four Kings and Queens in ensuring that Sahael, Alkebulan, and Aarde would be safe."

"Come," Oxossi said, waving toward the palace. "Such discussions can continue once all of you have eaten and rested. Our guards will take you to your quarters where you will feel the peace of this realm. Follow them and we will reconvene tomorrow over breakfast."

During the night, Aamira slept well despite Abioye's tossing and turning. By morning, her husband's wounds seemed much better, and he breathed easier. Adewara joined them and spoke of sitting against the monument quite bored the entire time they participated in the trials. Aamira laughed at the irritation in his voice.

While waiting for the Nubian Guard to arrive as their escort to breakfast, Aamira talked with her sons, discovering the terrors they faced on their trials, which seemed tailormade to prey on their fears and weaknesses. Yinká faced monstrous snakes, while Yekú, normally so successful in whatever idea he thought of, found every plan he came up with failing one after another. Yemí and Yomí related similar circumstances.

And yet, her boys had made it through. They were kings from their birth, and she loved them dearly.

The Nubian guards arrived, and the group left for breakfast. After thirty minutes of traveling, the escorts walked them to Nisine's giant feasting hall, a towering room with pillars on all sides that opened to a beautiful garden and a pleasant breeze.

The food was cooked, prepared, and brought to them so that they could eat and rest.

"Where is Sariah and Oxossi?" Abioye asked Aamira as he munched on bread with fruit spread on top. "It's been over an hour."

"I'm not sure," Aamira said, looking around the open hall for the rulers, noticing only Nubian Guards everywhere.

Adewara finished chewing a piece of apple. "It seems Oxossi and Sariah want us to stay here and not travel around this place at all. Last night I tried to explore around Nisine's palace, but the Nubian Guards forbade me from leaving my quarters. Before they stopped me, I saw multitudes of people behind these palace walls. I saw a man and woman that had eyes like Aamira and the boys."

"Why won't they allow us to see them?" Aamira asked

curiously.

"Another mystery," Adewara shrugged as he bit off a large piece of chicken.

After eating, they rested on the comfortable castle couches and relaxed. Musicians came and went, playing songs for the royal family, while lunch, and later dinner, were also provided.

Night fell and still no Oxossi and Sariah ever appeared. The guards lit torches to give light.

The night crept on.

Eventually the group fell asleep in the feasting hall as the stars looked down on them.

Aamira awakened in the middle of the night, startled. A few torches were still lit in the garden beyond the pillars, but other than that it was pitch black.

The Nubian guards were still on watch, preventing anyone from leaving the banquet chambers; Aamira walked up to one of them as if to exit into the garden, but the female soldier refused to let her pass.

Instead, Aamira started walking around the feasting hall, observing the images on the pillars. Carvings of the lineages that belonged to the chosen, sacred, divine, and cursed bloodlines stretched from floor to ceiling high above.

After an hour, footsteps caught Aamira's attention behind her. She turned to see a tall and muscular Nubian Guard escorting Abioye and Adewara, who were both rubbing sleep from their eyes.

"The three of you have been summoned. Follow me," The Nubian Guard said.

Aamira, Abioye, and Adewara followed the Nubian Guard out into the night until they approached a circle of stones expertly carved into pylons with rectangular stones over the tops forming what looked like twelve-foot-tall doorways. The stones glowed, illuminating the area despite the dark night.

"Welcome to the ancient Nabta gates," the guard said, motioning toward Oxossi and Sariah, who stood in the center of the large circle of stones, in front of a circular gateway made of pure Orichalcum.

"What is this place?" Aamira asked as she stepped toward the two rulers.

"These are the Nabta Gates," Sariah answered. "I think you already know what they do. Watch and see for yourself."

Navigators and Gate Guardians stood outside to the left and right of the ancient Nabta gates. Nibiru Gate Builders touched the Orichalcum ring, manipulating symbols like tiles on a child's puzzle box.

Oxossi pointed to the men and women running calculations on the gateway. "The Nibiru traveled throughout Aarde, building Nairohenge gates and Nabtahenge gates. The Nibiru constructed them all over Aarde to help Sahael govern and police the world. They ensured that all the black peoples in Aarde were taken care of and managed, before they fell into petty bickering and disputations amongst themselves. Look at the symbols at the top of the gateway."

Above them, at top of the Nabta gates, were four sigils: the Orisha, Yoruba, Hausa, and the Demir crests.

Suddenly, all four sigils lit up simultaneously.

"Now, as the symbols illuminate after the calculations of the Nibiru," Sariah said, "They allow travel to and from the Astral Realm. The monuments in Aarde are the only means of getting here. It was a secret that only Solomon the protector of Aarde, and the first Queens and Kings of Sahael knew about, a secret kept away from the Sahaelian House."

"Why have you come here, Aamira of Sahael?" Oxossi asked, looking her in the eyes. "We asked yesterday, and I would ask again."

"I have come to retrieve the heart of Inkalamu" Aamira said.

Sariah and Oxossi looked at each other and nodded.

"The heart of Inkalamu is yours to have for completing the watcher trials of Arishkegal and Enqi, your parents," Oxossi said. "They were the ones who created the trials for their children at the request of Kaimana and Kainoa, who deemed it crucial if they wanted access to their technology. If I may ask, what do you plan on doing with Inkalamu's heart?"

"I don't know," Aamira said as she looked up at the sky and rubbed the back of her neck. "I know it is needed to heal Neros's Realm, and thus all of Aarde, but I don't know how to do that. I was hoping you could tell us. I've been so focused on retrieving Inkalamu's heart, I didn't stop to think about what I would do once it was in my possession."

Oxossi reached behind his neck and pulled a necklace from beneath his robes. At the end of the chain was a green gemstone that looked as if it had cracked into several pieces.

"This is half of Inkalamu's heart," he said, handing it to Aamira. Sariah did the same, revealing she too wore a hidden gem; the second half of Inkalamu's heart, and gave it to Aamira.

Aamira's tattoos glowed brightly as she touched the pieces of jewelry. Kemite armor appeared all over her body. The pieces of Inkalamu's Heart pulled together as if attracted to a magnet, forming one single stone. Aamira placed the chains around her neck. Inkalamu's heart hung over her chest, glowing for all to see.

Adewara clapped his hands and smiled. "Now that we have Inkalamu's heart, we have a way to save Neros's Realm and the Nerosian people. Inkalamu's heart will be how we may be able to regain entry into Sahael as well."

Aamira remained quiet, looking down at the jewel around her neck. She had made a covenant with Steward Ọbalúayé and Stewardess Odùduwà that she and Abioye would take their place and remain in Neros's Realm for the rest of their lives to guarantee Aarde thrived. The stewards had given up their godhood to protect the people and would soon die. Aamira could not break her oath.

She would never get to see Sahael; only her sons and the Yoruban people would set foot on the sacred lands.

Abioye took her hand and nodded his head as if understanding her thoughts. A great love swelled in her chest as she looked into his eyes. Her husband was a good man. She could love him again, as she saw nothing but love in his eyes as they jointly contemplated a sacrifice that would define their lives together. Aamira and Abioye knew that Aarde needed them, and they needed to uphold their end of the agreement.

"We will never make it to Sahael," Abioye said.

Aamira then went on to explain the complex situation to Sariah and Oxossi, of how they offered to be stewards of Neros's Realm once they had completed their task in the Trials.

A broad smile filled Sariah's face. "Inkalamu's Heart consists of many Emerald pieces needed to help restore what's been lost in Neros's Realm and Sahael. Each of your family members are worthy of one of the six stones, as you earned them in your trials. We understand you and your sons need to be on your way back to Neros's Realm. Know, we hold you in the highest respect, even among angels and gods themselves."

Sariah raised her hand and ordered a Navigator and a Gate

Guardian from the circular structure of the Nabtahenge gates to help escort Aamira, Abioye, and Adewara back to Neros's realm. Another set of guards was dispatched to wake up the boys and gather them for the journey.

Within a few minutes Aamira, Abioye, Yinká, Yekú, Yemí, Yomí and Adewara all stood before the gates of Nabtahenge. The Navigator walked up to them and knelt. Oxossi and Sariah examined the elaborate design braided into the Navigator's hair and knew how to get them back to Neros's Realm.

"Now we will say goodbye to you, Royal family," Oxossi grinned. "Go with our blessing, and know, Ishtar and Obatala are with you, always."

An emerald portal opened in the center of the Orichalcum ring. A great wind blew, smelling of lavender and sage. The Medjay Gate Guardian entered the swirling electrical mass first.

The Navigator entered next, followed by Aamira and her family.

A warm tingle vibrated along her skin as she passed through the portal into darkness. The portal remained open behind them, silently churning. Aamira looked around, seeing they weren't in the center of Thebes as she expected, but rather a tunnel with smooth walls. Water dripped, echoing somewhere in the distance.

"Where are we?" Aamira asked.

"We're in Neros's caves," one of the Navigators answered.

"I thought we would return to the center of Nero's Realm, where the Nairohenge Gate is located," Abioye replied.

"No, my king," the Navigator continued. "That Gate has not been reactivated. We needed to access the tunnels here where we could manifest one of Nebuchadnezzar's Portals close to the

Realm.”

“I see,” Aamira said, disappointed they would still have a good distance to travel before returning to Thebes.

A quiet growl startled Aamira. She looked around in the dark.

“Mom, look!” Yekú laughed in his deep baritone.

Several short-haired bears lumbered toward them in the darkness. The same bears they had ridden through the tunnels in the first place.

“I knew they would find us again!” young Yinká said as he hugged the closest bear.

“The bears here can take us back to Thebes,” Adewara said. He patted one of the beasts and scratched behind its ear.

“Then we bid you farewell, King and Queen Adesola,” the Navigator said with a slight bow. The representatives of the Astral Plane then stepped back through the portal one by one, and the twisting mass of green energy closed behind them, plunging the tunnel into darkness. Aamira’s tattoos lit up without her even thinking about it, which in turn activated the green stones on the walls. Once again, the tunnels bathed the family in pale emerald light just as it had years ago on their journey to Neros’s Realm.

“Let’s go,” Aamira said. She climbed onto the back of the closest bear and grasped its fur for stability.

The bears ran swiftly, exiting the tunnels after a few hours. The family passed through the forest where bodies hung dead from the trees as they always had.

The trees seemed drier than usual though, as if a drought had struck the land. Leaves hung limp and desiccated, with some turning brown.

They passed the damaged gates of Thebes, seeing that the

work they had done to repair them remained despite the time loop the people lived in. The Nerosian people had done much to rebuild the city in their absence. Perhaps change was coming to Neros's Realm already.

The guards of the outer gate recognized Aamira immediately. They cheered and welcomed the royal family into the city. A battalion of guards acted as escorts through the streets. Citizens of Thebes waved and shouted as the royal family passed toward the halls of the Negrunde.

Within minutes, Aamira and her family rode into the center of Thebes where the Nairohenge gates were located beneath the cobblestone ground. Steward Ọbalúayé and Stewardess Odùduwà met them there with smiles on their faces. The Nerosian people circled the city circle and watched with expectant eyes.

"We welcome you back with open arms from the Watcher trials," Stewardess Odùduwà said. Her eyes fell on Aamira's chest, where the Heart of Inkalamu rested. "I see you have Inkalamu's Heart around her neck. Inkalamu's power is still intact and will keep Neros's Realm upright, with power flowing from Katunkumene through Neros's Realm to bless the Sahaelian and Alkebulan people."

"Change has already begun," Ọbalúayé grinned. "We feel free of our temporal prison, as do the people. It is a blessing for us to live in time once more."

Aamira and Abioye dismounted their bears along with their sons and Adewara.

"It is good to be back," Aamira said as she hugged Stewardess Odùduwà. "And it's good to see the both of you more alive and interactive than you have been over the past 16 years."

"You have no idea," Ọbalúayé chuckled.

"But we must now heal the realm and all of Aarde,"

Odùduwà said. "Look here to where the Nairohenge Gates lay hidden. This area in Neros's Realm has started to wither away and die slowly. This will indeed affect the seas, all wildlife and vegetation, and the skies above. The Heart of Inkalamu is the only hope for bringing life back to the realm and preventing Aarde from dying. Life will not spring from the ground unless magic once again runs through it."

Inkalamu's heart lit up suddenly as if in response to the Stewardess' words. It started to pulsate slowly. Aamira looked back at Steward Ọbalúayé and Stewardess Odùduwà for a sign of what she should do.

Abioye stepped toward the patch of dirt and started digging a small hole. He glanced toward Aamira and nodded for her to join him.

"What are you doing," she asked.

"They said nothing will grow unless magic flows through the soil," Abioye answered. He smiled. "I think it's pretty clear."

For the second time in as many days, Aamira felt a swell of love for her husband. He was proving himself to be far more thoughtful than he had in years past. The words he spoke on their journey to Nisine's Monument came back to her mind. *I want to fix it. I want to be with my wife again, smiling and making love like when we were young.*

She was certain she now wanted that too.

Aamira touched the Heart, feeling the individual pieces held together by magic. She pulled one of the six pieces from the others and held it in her hand. The small piece glowed. She placed that part of Inkalamu's Heart in the spot of dirt Abioye had dug and buried it several inches deep.

After a few moments, the spot of dirt changed.

What was once dry, hard, and dead started to fill with life.

Aamira and Abioye stood up together; as they did, the dirt all around Neros's Realm started to enliven. The soil revived, the Marula Trees throughout Neros's Realm regained their vitality. Dry leaves became green and lush.

The magical power from Inkalamu's Heart spread through Neros's forest, restoring life by feeding all the insects, animals, and the Nerosian people.

"The magical power throughout Neros's Realm has been brought back by a portion of Inkalamu's Heart," Stewardess Odùduwà said as the people cheered. "As joyous as this is, it still doesn't allow us the ability to enter Neolithic's chamber. We need Nzingha's Emerald key that is no longer in Neros's realm because of Captain Brooks."

"We will deal with it in time, but we need to get to Sahael first," Adewara said.

"Yes, but for now, let us rest and feast," Steward Ọbalúayé said as the people continued applauding and praising Ishtar all around them. The celebration could not be stopped.

The realm had been restored.

Everyone feasted.

As the festival commenced throughout the realm, the royal family ate with the Stewards in the place. After their meal and many musical numbers from talented performers, Stewardess Odùduwà took Aamira, Abioye, and Adewara aside into the garden.

"It's time for you all to rest before the transfer of power takes place," she said. "Neros's Realm will belong to you, King and Queen Adesola. The transfer will take place in a few months. We will provide you with the means of traveling to A.M.I.T."

"In Timbuktu?" Adewara asked, excitement in his voice.

"Yes," the Stewardess nodded. She looked at Aamira.

"You have taken upon yourself the responsibility of ruling this realm as your grandparents did. This is no small sacrifice, but know, Ishtar and Obatala always provide a way for their preparations to come to fruition, though even we lesser gods can't always comprehend their machinations. Be blessed, and rest until the journey."

Aamira and Abioye returned to their residence, saying goodnight to their sons and Adewara. Tomorrow would be another day, another journey, and another struggle,

But for tonight, the two lovers were content to rest in each other's arms, making love for the first time in many years; rekindling a passion they both thought long lost.

CHAPTER VIII
GLIMPSES OF THE PAST

Aarde, Nambissian Sea, A.M.I.T.

Two happy months passed in Neros's Realm. Aamira felt a restoration of joy. Her sons led the people of Thebes in a final push to rebuild the walls. The quakes here had ceased entirely, much to the bliss of a people restored to full life and vibrancy.

The Royal family traveled through Neros's newly rebuilt realm, visiting all five of the ancient halls. King and Queen Adesola, and their children, were followed by Nubian guards wherever they went. Adewara spent a lot of time in the Duwisib Palace library mainly in the archives, waiting for the transition of power to occur. Everyone in the Royal Family studied day and night, learning more about their past. Adewara wanted to see if they could discover any clues that might help them get closer to Sahael and their ancestors.

After several days of intensive studying and research something was discovered.

"I found something," Adewara said excitedly, as he ran up to everyone in the library reading area.

Yemí and Yomí closed their book quickly, as if happy to

have a distraction. Abioye, who had been chatting quietly with Yinká and Yekú, coughed and nodded his head toward Adewara as if telling his sons to pay attention.

"What did you find?" Aamira asked, putting down her book and sitting back on the comfortable couch behind her.

Adewara pointed to a text of nothing but hieroglyphic symbols. "It says here that Ishtar and Obatala sent down all their chosen blood, his brothers who were all kings, and his sisters who were all queens. The women it says searched out the best bloodlines to mingle with. They were the three Alkebulan Empires."

"You can read Hieroglyphics?" Aamira asked.

"Yes, during my postdoctoral at Timbuktu it was required. These are Dogon symbols. It took me awhile to translate them because they are an old dialect. The Dogon taught us their language and we taught them astronomy in turn. Follow me and I'll read the ancient writings being displayed across Nephrophida's interactive wall map that I just found."

The family stood and entered the hallway toward the second library section. Aamira had seen the hieroglyphs on the walls here for many years, but thought they were just decorations.

Pointing his finger at a thin line of hieroglyphic text, Adewara took a deep breath. "It took me some time to discover these symbols here because I wasn't looking for them. Then I read in one of the Dogon texts about hidden lines of symbols in important works of art, and I found these. It reads here that there was a problem; every bloodline in Alkebulan was strong, not a single origin was lesser than the other."

"Ishtar and Obatala must have done something about it," Aamira said.

"Ishtar and Obatala did," Adewara agreed. "The Queens

and the Kings randomly select bloodlines to mingle with, creating a robust and unbreakable bond with those Kings and Queens who would mix with the ancestries of the Alkebulan people. The Nectanebo Alliance formed out of these pacts, making them protectors over the three empires. Every black body, no matter where they were in Aarde, would be blessed by these actions."

"So, what you are saying is that these Kings and Queens mingled with the people and would search out all of these other tribes and because no tribe was inferior compared to the other?" Aamira asked.

Adewara nodded. "They were all superior, so the Chosen Bloodlines embraced them, their culture, language, and merged lineages with them."

Abioye stepped closer to the small line of carvings and squinted his eyes. "So basically, everyone in Alkebulan has the blood of a King or a Queen within them from the Chosen Ancient Royal lineage?"

"That's correct; it's why the Yoruba bloodline has the responsibility of saving all the black people in Aarde who share the royal lineage of Ishtar and Obatala. Lord Commander Natas wants to kill as many black men and traffic as many black women as he can. Every male and female with black skin shares this bloodline, and he wants to wipe it out."

"That's why he's wanted to enslave every black person," Aamira said, finally understanding the strange motivation to make black people slaves. "Deep down, he truly fears us. He fears the Katunkumene gene of royalty."

Abioye put his arm around his wife. "These Kings and Queens made their lineages stronger and are the backbones of each of their respective heritages. Ishtar and Obatala commanded them to multiply and replenish the sacred bloodlines of Kings and

Queens in Alkebulan,"

"That is right," Adewara said. "That was the prophecy sent from Andalusia to populate Alkebulan."

"Tell us what happened next," Aamira urged.

"Follow me to a section in the palace archives that are off-limits to the Nerosian people," Adewara said.

The Royal family followed him to the scholar's quarters, a room with a locked door that Adewara opened by whispering a word. They stepped inside a round room with towering ceilings. While not large, the chamber featured opulent windows and pillars that reached up to a colorful mosaic on the ceiling of gods in the middle of Aarde's creation. A round table sat on stone tiles, covered in metal plates and scrolls of velum.

"I found the password to this room during my studies," Adewara said. "I learned that after several hundred centuries of living in Alkebulan, the royal bloodlines grew to hundreds of millions of people. One day they were all summoned by the Sahaelian House to figure out how to initiate the first gathering in Sahael." Adewara sat down at the table, looking over ancient sea scrolls. He grabbed one and opened it.

Aamira bent over and looked at the words on the scroll. They were in a language she couldn't read.

"The First Gathering. That's a term I've heard several times," Yemí said as he rubbed his beard thoughtfully.

Adewara nodded. "The Sahaelian House, after they had sanctioned the first gathering, sanctioned a second gathering of the blood-bound rights to take place in Alkebulan. The Sahaelian House ushered in the Blood Rights, Blood Oaths, Blood Bonds, and Blood Vows before the Blood Wars."

"What were the Blood Wars?" Abioye asked. I've never

heard of them. Were they among the Sahaelian and Alkebulan peoples?"

"The Alkebulan Blood Wars were to allow the second gathering to take place," Adewara read.

"To take place?" Yomí asked.

"Yes. Unfortunately, the Narsans invaded Sahael city, Aardian city, and Alkebulan city, destroying all three. The Ancient Bloodlines of the motherland were enslaved and taken away from their ancestral homeland."

"Are we discussing Sahael or Alkebulan?" Aamira asked.

"Alkebulan," Adewara said.

"Why would anyone want to disrupt the bloodlines on the motherland?" Abioye questioned.

Adewara continued. "The Tribes of Alkebulan were all displaced and dispersed, sent to other lands full of witans that were foreign to them. If you take a look at Nephrophida's Interactive Map, you'll see three Alkebulan empires."

Aamira felt soreness in her throat and lungs as she imagined how the people were stolen against their own free will and transported to the Nations in Western Aarde as enslaved people.

She swallowed. "This is all the work of Lord Commander Natas and the Narsans, who Invaded Sahael, her three cities, and destroyed Khartoum Palace."

"The Narsans made it a point to enslave the most prominent Alkebulan Bloodlines in the three Empires of Songhai, Axum, and Kush," Adewara continued. "Lord Commander Natas sent them to western Aarde to be enslaved until their dying days."

"Perhaps we could save them," Prince Yekú said. "After all, that's why we've done everything since we were children.

Mother left her home on the Estate to free the people."

"I agree," young Yinká added. "We know Natas destroyed Sahael, and that the entire Alkebulan continent is poisoned. This information is nothing new. All we need to do is lead the people, and the witans will be overthrown."

"That's the point I'm trying to make," Adewara continued. "Lord Commander Natas sent the Sahaelian bloodlines to the provinces to work them to death. Those that survived would be sent to the outer lands like IFF to be hunted for the rest of their lives. Then Lord Commander Natas sent the Alkebulan Bloodlines from Songhai, Axum, and Kush in Western Aarde. He did this to slowly eradicate the sacred blood and the Alkebulan bloodline to keep and control the population, ensuring he had total control of their lives."

"Again, we know all of this," Yemí said, folding his muscular arms.

Adewara took a deep breath. "The people who once called Sahael home, the people who were the most powerful in all Aarde, have now lived for two generations in captivity. They no longer have the same will they once had. They will not simply follow you and fight. Many of them won't, anyway, because they only know enslavement now. It is not a simple thing to pull people out of a mindset that they have known their entire existence. They are lost, and we have no idea where to start to pull them up again. Do you have any idea how many Alkebulans remained on IFF and enslaved? People who had the chance to come to the safety of Karnak and be free, but that stayed behind because it was the life they had always known? Tens of thousands."

Aamira had never thought of it from this angle before. She just assumed everyone would join her and her cousins when the time came.

"How can we help them if we don't know where to start?" Abioye said, voice quiet.

"Is there anything else?" Aamira asked. "If this information is so important, there must be some detail about breaking that cycle."

Adewara flipped to the end of the Neros scrolls. "No, that's where the information ends; all that is left is this Inscription. Most of the text here warns that there will not be enough people to join in the redemption of Sahael. Some tribes are hidden and will have no idea the gathering is taking place. Others will not heed the call, which means Natas will conquer once again no matter what we do."

"That can't be," Aamira said.

"The Signs of the Times are a warning for the blooded tribes to go into hiding," Adewara read. "The final inscription reads; *They are to wait for the ancient bloodlines to find them and help get them get to Sahael. They must be awakened."*

The royal family spent the next hour talking about what Adewara had told them. The Educator left for a time but returned with the evening meal so they could continue their discussion.

"Before we get to Sahael, we need to find a way to help achieve the first gathering of the twelve," Aamira said as she ate some grapes. "These sacred bloodlines need searching out. Once found, only then can we complete the first gathering, ordered by the Sahaelian House."

Yemí grabbed a few dried dates and tossed them in his mouth. "That is why we need to travel to Timbuktu, as the Steward and Stewardess implied."

"But Mom and Dad can't leave Neros's Realm once they are made Emperor and Empress," Yinká replied.

"I agree with Yemí," Yomí said. "Once in Timbuktu we can know what to do about helping complete the gathering and inspiring more people to escape captivity. We can help restore Sahael and figure out what to do next at that point."

After a few more hours had passed, Ọbalúayé and Odùduwà came down to the archives to inform them that Empress and Emperor Adesola were the new rulers of the realm.

"You now possess all the power within Neros's Realm," Stewardess Odùduwà said. "In addition, Sariah and Oxossi are now in control of Neros's realm until Empress and Emperor Adesola are able to return."

Aamira and Abioye looked at each other, confused.

"I thought there would be a ceremony, or something," Abioye said.

"And what do you mean by 'return?'" Aamira asked. "I thought the whole point was that we could never leave once instated as the Emperor and Empress."

"It's time we explained everything to you," Stewardess Odùduwà said. "Every Alkebulan is imbued with the power to know who they are as people. The ancient blood within them needs to be awakened to help restore Sahael; once the four bloodlines have returned to Sahael you all will understand the Signs of the Times."

"That's what we were just talking about," Yekú said. "We don't know how to awaken the people, or what that even means."

Steward Ọbalúayé waved his hands in the air, conjuring a glowing interactive map of Aarde. Pale blue light shone in the chamber and reflected off the windows.

"Wow," Yemí breathed.

"Now that my wife and I are no longer stuck in the

temporal loop, our abilities can manifest once more," the Steward informed. "This map has specific marked locations that you are unaware of. It is deep knowledge we now share with you."

Aamira and Abioye looked closely at the map. Aamira noticed the markings of sigils showing where the other sacred bloodlines were located.

"It would appear that we're going to have to find them and travel to those locations?" Abioye asked.

"You see the wall dividing Eastern and Western Aarde," Odùduwà said, pointing at a black line running down the center of the map. "This is a giant wall built by the ancients. Nibiru's wall has always been undergoing constant repairs. It can be crossed if you know where these weak spots are located. Traveling to Timbuktu will help you acquire the information and knowledge needed to change the course of history forever for good by disrupting witan power and restoring the black power structure on Aarde."

"You make it sound easy," Yomí grumbled.

"Indeed, the witan power structure will fight tooth and nail to stay at the top," Odùduwà said.

Steward Ọbalúayé stared at the map. "The invasion of the Narsans and the Ennead have set up events that are now taking place around Aarde. The Signs of The Times are designed to provide the chosen bloodlines with the time they need to get to Sahael. The quakes, the forming and destroying of mountains, the breaking of the land, substances of hot liquid coming up out of the continents killing everything they touched. These events are triggered by the Black Madonna's to prevent them from being tracked and followed."

The Steward's words reminded Aamira of whispers from the past.

"In my first meeting with Solomon," Aamira began, "he told me and my sisters the signs are designed to keep us safe until we all reach Sahael. Apparently, we need to continue doing our part and hope that we can get there. Now I hope too that our people will actually follow us to freedom and not stay chained even when their bonds are broken."

Adewara stood from behind the table and stretched his back. "We need to find a way to Timbuktu if we want any chance of surviving on the Alkebulan continent."

"We know," Stewardess Odùduwà said. "And no redemption can be complete without the Princess of the Yoruban line standing at the head with her sisters."

"What are you saying?" Aamira asked. "You've told us many times over the past 16 years that we can never leave Neros's Realm once we become Emperor and Empress."

"And that was true," Ọbalúayé agreed, "for your grandparents."

Aamira blinked. "I don't understand."

Stewardess Odùduwà smiled. "For the 16 years you were with us, we were constantly repeating what was told to your grandparents. Yes, the circumstances mirror the present, but we could not deviate too much from the cycle of time. Now, as Sahael's redemption nears, such rules are no longer applicable. The key that was taken needs to be recovered, and only the Yoruban Royal family can do it for reclamation to take place."

"Now that the transfer of power is complete, you can leave the realm as a family," Steward Ọbalúayé said. The map disappeared as he dropped his arms and laughed. "Strange times have passed, and now we can all look forward to a brighter future. You are the rulers of Neros's Realm, but this plane of existence will thrive now, awaiting your eventual return."

Aamira laughed as well. "So, we can go together? I thought we were going to have to send the boys as our proxies!"

Stewardess Odùduwà placed a hand on Aamira's shoulder. "Family is always stronger together, and yours is one of the strongest I've ever seen."

CHAPTER IX
A.M.I.T

Vannadale pass, Nambissian Sea, AMIT

After a few days, the Royal Family was ready and prepared to leave. Adewara studied maps and plotted a course that would lead them to Timbuktu.

They all congregated at the shores of Neros's Realm, where the ocean waves crashed against a timeless shore.

Ọbalúayé and Odùduwà had prepared a ship small enough to keep Aamira and her family hidden as they traveled on the seas. It was captained by Admiral Abdul, a six-foot-eight-inches tall man with long dreaded gray hair and a Black Orichalcum long riffle he kept on himself at all times. He wore nicely knitted rogue clothing and seemed to be in his early 40's.

They loaded themselves onto the ship with a small crew of sailors chosen because of their courage and fortitude. The Steward and Stewardess stood on the shore, bidding the royal family farewell.

"May your travels be safe!" Steward Ọbalúayé cried.

"May Sahael be your destination, and the prophecies be

fulfilled that our people will once again find refuge!" Odùduwà shouted with a smile.

The ship then set off on the calm ocean currents traveling east, then north, and then west on the way to the island of A.M.I.T and then to the city of Timbuktu.

The Royal family sailed for months, navigating through the Vannadale pass, avoiding the patrolling Dalean ships on the shores, and in the waters. Adewara was constantly vigilant, always on the bow of the ship with a telescope watching the horizon for any potential dangers.

A strange tension settled on the boat. Every other ship they passed could potentially be the one that discovered their true natures as royalty. Aamira had gotten used to the safety of Neros's Realm, as had her sons. Now with danger everywhere, the sheer act of staying vigilant became exhausting.

"To avoid the patrolling ships, we have to enter the Nautical Pass," Adewara said one afternoon.

"Is that dangerous?" Yekú asked as he tightened a rope attached to the main sail.

"I've heard of the Nautical Pass before," Aamira said, eyes still focused on the ocean in front of them. "But I know nothing about it."

"It's what the Narsans created to trade goods, minerals, and resources," Adewara said.

"You're going to have to be more specific than that," Aamira said.

"I assure you, that you and your family will see it all with your own eyes," Adewara said. He walked toward the back of the ship, carrying his telescope.

Yekú walked up to his mother and leaned against the

wooden guardrail. "Does that mean it's dangerous or not?"

"You know better than to ask an Educator a simple question," she shrugged.

The following morning, the Royal Family entered the Nautical Pass, staying close to the shores of Kumasi, entering the circular trade. Ships of all sizes filled the pass. Dozens of vessels jockeyed for position with sailors shouting and cursing all around. The Nero ship became surrounded by other larger boats and ferries.

Everyone gathered on the ship's prow where they could see the pandemonium all around them. Adewara took a deep breath.

"We're going to have to wait for an opening to avoid not causing disruption and bringing unnecessary attention to us in any way whatsoever," Admiral Abdul said. He looked at the four boys and nodded his head toward the back of the ship. "Let's all get back to work on the riggings and any jobs that need to be done. We're a traveling merchant vessel. Nothing more. We don't want to be inspected and potentially destroyed when they find out who we are."

The ship traveled slowly to maintain the specific speed required of all vessels entering the Nautical trade. After a few hours, the logjam loosened, and ships passed through. The Nero ship was waved along by a patrolling freighter and ordered to continue toward Dorth pass.

The Royal Family and Adewara waited until they distanced themselves from the ships behind them and in front of them. When Admiral Abdul knew it was safe, they exited the Nautical route, entering the Dorth pass smoothly. A few days later they docked their ship in the hidden port at Dorth and resupplied.

The sea and the lands were in total disruption all around them. Typhoons, sinkholes, and whirlpools had battered the landscape. The port itself was a mess of garbage and debris. Rain poured down adding to the overall melancholy of the moment.

"What happened here?" Aamira asked a fisherman as he tugged at his torn nets from beneath an overturned boat.

"Storms," the man growled as he rubbed his graying beard and wiped rain from his dark forehead. "Nothin' but storms. They've prevented all ships from traveling through the pass to avoid what's happenin' in the open waters. I'd turn back if I was you. Even stayin' here ain't wise. Waves wreck everything the last few months. Best head back where's you came from."

The Royal Family rested at an Inn in upper Dorth port, the city where travelers and smugglers took refuge to rest and wait for their ship to be repaired and fully stocked once more. Admiral Abdul and his men, along with Adewara, stayed with the ship.

Aamira and the family shared a single room, with the boys sleeping on the floor. Wind blew tirelessly outside throughout the night, making it hard to sleep.

What would they do? It seemed the Signs of the Times were getting worse, not better. How many ships had sunk, and sailors drowned in the past few months alone? How many refugees died trying to sail to a better life?

As Aamira stared up at the dark ceiling listening to Abioye breathing quietly, the floorboards squeaked. She raised her head enough to see young Yinká, her youngest child, stand and look out the window. He looked around quickly and snuck out of the room.

Where are you going, young man? Aamira asked herself. *Wherever it is, you're only 17. You're not going alone.*

Aamira slowly creeped out of bed and into the hallway. She walked down the stairs, amidst the multitude of people who sat at tables and the bar drinking away their sorrows. At least the tavern was doing well financially through all the devastation. They must be going through liquor by the barrel.

Aamira stepped out the front door into the dark and wet night. The rain had stopped, but the wind continued to howl. The streets were muddy and cold.

Down the street she saw Yinká stepping slowly toward an alleyway. He seemed like a cat on the prowl, shoulders hunched and limbs tight like a spring ready to release. She followed him down the alley and to the outskirts of the village where light from fires gleamed through the trees in a forested area. Something was going on out here, and it didn't feel like a simple campout. Yinká had seen something out the window before he stepped out; something bad.

"What are you doing out here?" a voice whispered in Aamira's ear. She jumped and turned to see her other three boys, faces barely visible in the light of the nearby fires. She swatted Yekú, who was the closest, across the shoulder.

"Why did you sneak up on me like that?" she whispered angrily. "You almost gave me a heart attack."

"We saw you leave and noticed Yinká was gone too," Yemí said quietly. "We wanted to see what was up. Now we're cold with all the wind. I wish I'd stayed in my blanket."

Aamira shook her head. "Well, if you're going to be here, stick close to me and let's keep following Yinká. I know that boy, and he wouldn't sneak out unless he thought it was something important."

The boys followed their mother closer to the fires. There, behind a tree watching something in the clearing beyond, stood Yinká. Aamira could now see more clearly what her boy was watching. Witan, Narsan men, and women were preparing to hang a group of eight black children. Several of the kids cried as a witan man yelled at them to shut up.

Aamira gasped, drawing Yinká's attention. The young man turned, eyes going wide as he saw his mother and brothers.

"What're you doing here?" Prince Yekú asked as he stepped over to Yinká.

"I saw a group of boys and girls with their hands tied outside the inn being taken somewhere," Yinká said. "I wanted to check it out since I couldn't sleep. What are *you* doing here?"

"Don't take that tone with me, young man," Aamira said, moving closer to the tree to get a closer look at the fires and potential hanging victims. "We saw you exciting the room. You think I wouldn't follow? Or your brothers? You should have woken us up instead of going out on your own. We're in enemy territory here for all intents and purposes. You draw attention to yourself and you're putting a target on your back. You understand?"

"I couldn't let anything bad happen to these kids," Yinká argued.

"What's wrong with their backs?" Yomí asked. He pointed at several of the kids who had what looked like small appendages sprouting out of their shoulder blades.

"My god," Aamira whispered. "The children had wings on their backs that have been clipped, preventing them from flying off and getting away. They must be of my cousin Heziara's bloodline; the Hausans. Adewara has shown me paintings of such children, but I've never---"

One of the witan men in the clearing shouted and swore as one of the little girls bit his arm. He raised a sword and went to bring it down on the girl's head.

Before Aamira had even noticed his movement, Yinká leaped forward, forming a green energy Glaive blade in his hand and stopping the sword before it hit its mark. The witan's mouth opened in surprise, but Yinká severed the man's head from his shoulders before a sound exited his throat.

"We're under attack!" another witan soldier screamed while pointing at Yinká.

"I guess we're fighting now," Yekú smiled. He and his brothers rushed forward, killing all the witans within seconds.

Aamira couldn't help but be impressed. She hadn't even needed to conjure her own blade. She still thought of them as children, but even Yinká was a man now for all intents and purposes.

Pride filled her chest as she walked over and began untying some of the children.

"It's going to be okay," Aamira whispered as the children cried. "You're safe now."

"They're all dead!" a little girl said, pointing at the bodies now littering the ground.

"That's a good thing, little one," Yemí replied as he untied several children.

Yekú hurried over to Aamira, pointing his glowing Glaive past the fires and into the dark forest. "Torches. I can see them through the trees. More witans are coming. We better get these kids out of here and keep moving. We can kill ten men no problem, but who knows how many are about to arrive here."

"Let's go," Aamira nodded. "Boys! Each of you take two of these children in your arms so we can move fast!"

"Yes, mother," Yinká said as he scooped up two of the kids under his arms and began running back toward town.

After a few minutes though, Aamira noticed more torches coming from the village. Apparently, a large group had planned to watch the hanging of these children.

"Dart to the west!" Aamira ordered her boys. They shifted course, coming to a cliff face that looked up at the stars. Blinking her eyes twice, Aamira activated her dark vision, seeing a cave a few yards ahead. She ducked inside swiftly, followed by her sons and the eight children.

Once inside the cave, the young boys and girls thanked Yinká and his brothers for saving them.

"Who are you?" one of the young girls asked.

"We are the princes of Yoruban House," Yemí answered. "And this is our mother, Queen Aamira."

"We're the children of Ikegwuru," one of the boys said, rubbing his clipped wings.

"Who is Ikegwuru?" Yekú asked.

"She is the goddess of all forests in Aarde," another girl said. "We were captured and had our wings clipped by our captors."

"How can we get you back to your parents?" Yinká asked.

"It's impossible for us to fly," the little girl said.

"Are we safe?" another boy asked.

Yinká nodded his head but looked to his mother. *"Are they really safe?"* he asked telepathically.

"As safe as they can be," Aamira replied. *"We need to see what is going on outside the cave. Boys, we need to use our abilities to see through the eyes of the animals in the forest. They will show us what's happening."*

The four brothers used their abilities to communicate and see through the eyes of the animals, as did Aamira. She saw soldiers trudging through the forest. She saw massive Lope Mastiff dogs smelling the ground and barking toward the cave in the distance.

She heard the barks with her own ears.

The damn dogs were close.

"Mastiffs," Yemí spat.

"Less than a quarter mile away," Yekú agreed. "They'll be here in minutes. They can smell us, and the children."

"We'll have to fight the Narsan forces if they find the entrance to the cave," Yemí said.

Aamira continued looking through the eyes of the animals. The Narsans found the dead slavers and immediately scoured the forest using Lope Mastiffs to sniff any scent out of the ordinary. The Lope's immediately picked up on the trail left behind by the fleeing Yorubans.

"They'll be here in a few minutes," Aamira whispered. The children began crying, hugging each other. A pang tugged at Aamira's stomach for their worry. Here they had thought they were going to die, only to be rescued, but now thrown back into the same fear as before. To a child, the trauma must be immense.

"We'll protect you," Yinká promised, soothing one of the little girls.

Aamira stood. "We have to think fast and ready ourselves to fight off a large pack of tamed monstrous dogs. Children, you will all stay here in the cave. Yes, it's dark, but you will be safe. My sons and I are no mere weak gathering of warriors like the witans. We are royalty of Sahael, trained for protection and the destruction of our enemies. You will live to see morning; of that I have no doubt."

The four brothers exited the cave with their mother as the sound of approaching dogs grew louder.

"You ever kill a Mastiff before?" Yekú asked Aamira with

a smile.

"I have not," she replied as her green armor formed over her body.

Yekú shrugged as his armor manifested as well. "It's going to be a memorable night for all of us then."

Sixteen Lope Mastiffs suddenly burst through the trees, slobber reflecting in the cold moonlight. They growled ferociously.

Egyptian glaives formed in the boys' hands as Aamira conjured a Glaive scythe. "Get ready everyone," Aamira said. "No quarter will be given."

All sixteen of the Lope Mastiffs attacked simultaneously. Aamira stepped back to guard the cave entrance, allowing her sons first crack at the beasts.

Yomí, who charged directly at the slobbering Mastiffs, contorted his body in a circular motion in mid-air. He spun with his glaive and sliced the heads off four Lope Mastiffs as both of his feet touched the ground once more.

Prince Yekú stood his ground. He modified his Egyptian glaive, making it a chain glaive, allowing him to attack them from a distance. Throwing half of his chained glaive at one of the Lope Mastiffs, the blade struck the dog's stomach and split its intestines onto the ground as the creature yelped. Yekú retracted the chain glaive, pulling it quickly from the stomach of the dead Lope and cutting a second Lope through the mouth and severing half its head. He then turned as two more Mastiffs charged, impaling themselves on Yekú's glaives, piercing their brains as they opened their mouths to attack.

Two more Lope Mastiffs charged Yemí from the front, and then two others stormed him from his right and left side adjacently. Yemí walked toward the two charging Mastiffs with his Egyptian glaive and broke it into two swords. The first two Mastiffs charged him but died on the point of his swords as he pirouetted in a full circle, slicing them in half from their head to their tails.

During his half pirouette, Prince Yemí severed the heads of the other two Lope Mastiffs. As well.

Not to be outdone by his older brothers, young Yinká bent down on both of his knees as four more dogs converged on him from all sides. He placed his right hand in the center of his glaive and split the face of the first Mastiff, who fell back yelping in pain. Yinká then swung the blade back behind him to divide the head of the second Mastiff. Swinging from right to left, he sliced the other Lope Mastiffs before standing back to his feet.

The four brothers had killed all sixteen Lope Mastiffs within seconds.

Yekú grabbed Yinká by the shoulder and grinned. "I've got to say little brother, Yomí spinning in the air and killing the dogs was pretty impressive, but you just kneeling and letting them come at you? I had chills."

So had Aamira. Watching her boys fight with such impressive skill filled her with pride. But Yinká's actions had been so thoughtful and precise, she understood why he would be called High King and rule over even his older brothers. The boy was something truly special.

"Back in the cave," Aamira ordered. "Hopefully with the dogs dead, the Witans will get lost in the forest. They're stupid to rely solely on animals for their tracking."

As they entered the cave, it was dark no longer. A pale white light filled the space.

"What is that light?" Yinká asked.

"Are these kids magic or something?" Yemí questioned as he shielded his eyes.

As Aamira's eyes adjusted to the glare, she saw a woman standing with the children. She stood seven feet tall with white hair, green eyes, dark chocolate unblemished skin and ivory teeth. Her frame was slender and muscular. Great bird wings sprouted from her back and wrapped around the children like a blanket.

"Ikegwuru," Aamira whispered.

"The goddess of the forest?" Yomí gasped.

Ikegwuru smiled and nodded to the royal family. "I want to thank the five of you for saving and defending my children with your lives." Ikegwuru spread her right hand and fingers apart and coughed into her hand. A symbol appeared on her palm. She then walked up to Yinká and placed her right hand around his neck and then removed it. The same symbol from her palm now glowed on his throat.

"I sense your power as a High King of Sahael," Ikegwuru said as she stared at Yinká. "I have given you a gift that only a goddess can provide a King. It is the Gift of Shout. This moment was foreordained."

The Gift of Shout. Aamira had read about this gift before. Its power was devastating, and it would call to the lost sheep of the Yoruban house from around the world. Her other sons may not quite understand, but for all intents and purposes Yinká had just been crowned their ruler.

"I thank you all again for saving my children," Ikegwuru said. "But more soldiers are coming. I sense their anger at the deaths of those you killed in the clearing. They are sending for reinforcements. I can help you get away. Follow me deep inside this cave."

A light formed in Ikegwuru's hand as she led the children and Aamira's family deeper into the cave. She stopped a few minutes later in a tall chamber filled with stalactites and dripping water. Rubbing the ring on her finger, a swirl of sparks and color appeared.

"This is one of Nebuchadnezzar's portals," she said. "It will allow you to return to wherever you wish. You need only conjure the thought."

"The boat?" Yomí asked.

"Our room at the inn," Aamira confirmed. "Your father is likely worried about all of us."

The four brothers nodded before walking through the portal and arriving in their shared room in the Inn. Aamira stepped through last, thanking the Goddess for her aid.

"Thank *you*, Daughter of Sahael," Ikegwuru replied. "I sense your path has moved from selfishness to courage. Your sons are a testament to your progression."

Aamira entered the room just as the portal closed, plunging them into darkness once more. Rain pattered against the window. The only other sound was snores coming from the bed where Abioye lay, seemingly oblivious to what his family had gone through over the past few hours.

"Is Dad still asleep?" Yekú asked.

"It looks that way," Aamira said, shaking her head.

"Should we let him keep sleeping?" Yomí chuckled.

Aamira shook her head. "No. We know the Narsans will be looking for who killed the slavers. We need to head back to the ship now and set off."

While groggy, Abioye packed quickly, listening intently as the boys and his wife took turns telling him what had happened. They ran into the freezing rain, making their way to the ship where Adewara slept on the deck.

He was not happy at the news they delivered.

"Hurry and get the boat ready for launch," Adewara said as he tossed ropes toward the main mast. "You boys must be more careful. You put Sahael and Aarde in danger of never seeing the great empire rise from the ashes once more. I'm glad you are okay, but I have a responsibility to Solomon, the protector of Aarde, and a promise to keep ensuring you all make it to Sahael safely. I must get all of you to A.M.I.T and to the city of Timbuktu."

"Should we light the torches so we can have more light?" Yemí asked as Adewara continued piling ropes on the deck.

"No," the Educator warned. "Use your dark vision. We don't want to draw any unwanted attention. Hopefully we can slip out before sunrise, and no one will be the wiser. Get the sails back up. Go!"

Aamira walked up to Adewara as the boys and Abioye scrambled across the deck following his orders.

"They were never in any real danger," Aamira said as she tied one of the ropes in place. "I was there with them the whole time."

"And had the goddess Ikegwuru not arrived, what would you have done then?" Adewara asked. "A few Lope Mastiffs are no danger, but an entire army? Don't let yourself be lulled into a false sense of your own abilities, Empress Adesola. There is too much at stake for your sons to wander off at night in enemy territory. They were blessed tonight, Yinká in particular, but that doesn't change the fact that death just as easily could have claimed them."

"What promise did you make to Solomon?" Aamira asked. "You mentioned a promise before when yelling at the boys. You've never spoken of it before."

"I was tasked with the responsibility of getting you all to

Sahael," Adewara said. "Solomon ordered it of me. I'm not at liberty to discuss or share any more than that."

"What do we do now?"

"We set sail. It should be another three days until we reach A.M.I.T. I have no idea what to expect there. It's possible there will be blockades from witan forces, or even all out warfare. Things on this trip have been easy in comparison to what we may find of the shores of the Educator lands."

The next three days were slow on the seas. Rain continued falling constantly, with many ships using the same currents as Aamira and her family. Some were obviously fine merchant vessels brimming with expensive silks and spices. Others rode heavy on the water with iron cannons and military units on the decks standing at attention.

The night before their arrival in A.M.I.T., cannon fire echoed constantly.

In the morning, fog covered the water thick enough to obscure all vessels. Explosions reverberated close by. Adewara sent one of the sailors on a skiff to determine what was going on. An hour later, the seaman returned and climbed back onboard.

"Sir," the man said, back straight. "Ships are firing cannons on the shoreline. Several forts line the cliffs, which are firing back. Any ship caught in between is being attacked by both sides. The water is thick with debris."

Adewara rubbed his beard. "Set our course to run wide of the battle. Where we want to enter is farther south anyway. We will look for the royal song caves. Hopefully, we can find them through the fog.”

“We need to find a way to avoid the ships attacking A.M.I.T,” Admiral Abdul said.

The Royal Family and Adewara traveled around the mountain structure avoiding the attacking ships. After several hours, the sounds of battle dulled, though the fog remained thick.

“Bring us closer to the cliffs,” Adewara ordered. “We need to see details, not just the darkness of the rock through the fog.”

“Sir, we could run aground if we get too close,” one of the sailors warned.

“At this point, if we don’t find what we’re looking for, we’re in trouble anyway,” Adewara said. “After spending nearly, a half-day avoiding the other ships, our luck isn’t likely to hold.”

As they sailed closer to the cliffs, large knives of rock came into view all around them. The sailors tugged on the rigging to pull the ship away from danger, but several times rocks smashed against the hull, leaving behind deep gouges and the sound of wood weeping against stone.

“There!” Adewara shouted, pointing toward an opening in the rock on their left.

“It looks like a crevice, with something on it,” Abioye said.

“Perhaps we should get closer,” Aamira replied.

The ship slowed and pulled closer to the opening in the rock. A symbol was carved above the crevasse in the mountain, emanating a Zambian glow.

“It’s a Sahaelian crest with Sahael’s sigil on it,” Adewara said.

“What does that mean?” Admiral Abdul asked.

"It means it's an entrance into the mountain of song, allowing entry to those of the Chosen bloodline," Adewara said.

The ship slammed into a rocky outcropping, throwing Aamira forward slightly in surprise.

"Let's not destroy the ship, shall we?" Yemí said as he steadied himself on his feet. Waves hit the side and pushed the ship against the rocks again.

"We'll need to abandon the boat for now," Adewara said. "The hidden passage you see is a Nabta entrance created in secret, centuries ago by the ancient Kemites to allow their bloodlines the ability to store and preserve their history. The Kemites did this, ensuring that their history would always be remembered and easily accessible to the chosen bloodlines. The Kemites wanted to make sure their posterity would remember their history. The Kemite history is rich. It has been taken away from the enslaved, enabling their witan oppressors to manipulate and control the flow of information, allowing them to keep the upper hand."

The sailors threw ropes around the jagged rocks and held the boat in place. Adewara climbed out first, followed by Abioye, Aamira, and finally the four boys.

"Keep the ship anchored here as best you can," Adewara ordered the sailors. "I have no idea how long this will take but stay here until you are close to running out of food. You should have enough for at least a month's time. Be honorable and serve your emperor and empress well."

"Yes sir," they all repeated.

The royal family followed Adewara along the rocks, walking deeper into the crevasse. Everything was wet and slippery, with mist flying in their faces from the wind and waves.

"Look!" Yekú said, pointing at more illuminated symbols carved on the dark rock cliffs. "Some of these symbols are glowing green too. What does it mean?"

Adewara paused and wiped water from his forehead. He placed his hand on one of the sigils. "After Timbuktu was built, the Ancient Kemites reached out to the watchers and provided them with a way to travel to A.M.I.T. That knowledge was kept with one of the twelve ancient tribes. This knowledge was essential to the survival of Sahael and to the Alkebulan people, who they are all here for to serve and protect at all costs."

They hiked further, coming directly under the large symbol at the crest of the crevasse depicting the eye of Horus in the base of the Marula Tree.

"This is as far as the crevasse goes," Abioye said, patting his hand against the rock. "Unless the entrance is under water, we're going to have to go back to the ship."

Shaking his head, Adewara placed his hand against the rock as well. "There is magic here. And science."

"What do we do?" Aamira asked. She had seen enough barriers fall away to know that with the right word or blood, even rock could fall away.

A wave smashed nearby, sending thick mist over them. Aamira wiped her hair from her forehead as water dripped from her nose.

"What do we do?" she asked again.

"I don't know," Adewara answered. "I've never come this way before. I assumed the rock would open once we arrived and interacted with the symbol above."

Aamira touched the rock as well, pushing against it with her hands. She could feel the power of the ocean vibrating in the stone. She focused on that vibration, closing her senses to all other sound and sensation. The ocean pounded relentlessly, spitting foam and salt into their faces. Still, Aamira touched the rock. What did the rock want? Was it blood? Sacrifice? What?

"The rock is vibrating slightly," Yomí said as he stood next to his mother.

"I noticed that," Aamira replied.

"Wait, didn't you say this was the mountain of song, or something like that?" Yekú asked.

Adewara paused. "I did. This crevasse is known in the writings for its resonant tone. Ancient choirs would come here to sing, as their voices would be amplified by the natural contours of the cave."

Yinká placed his hand on the rock as well and began to hum.

"What are you doing?" Abioye asked.

"Trying to match the tone of the rock," Yinká answered. "Perhaps that is what the entrance needs; a matching note."

Aamira grinned. Her son was truly creative and intelligent. She followed his lead, placing her hand on the stone one more time and humming to match the frequency she felt in her fingers. Soon all of them hummed in unison, creating a note that seemed to grow in volume until it echoed through the cave and overcame the crashing ocean behind them.

Suddenly, the rock began to fold in on itself, opening wide and letting the water rush in.

"It's opening!" Adewara cried. "A path in the water will take us there. Head back to the ship!"

And thus, they did. The sailors, who had been content to wait a month until they ran out of food, were overjoyed at the royal families return. They untied the ropes, and the ship slipped into the entrance of the mountain of song. Large gusts of severe wind roared up behind them, directing their ship deeper into the mountain.

Then, as if like a dream, the rock disappeared above them and sunlight filtered down onto the deck. Warm air replaced the constant moistness of the outer shores. The water flowed along a forest of Marula trees that grew directly out of the ocean itself. They still appeared to be inside a cave, but by some magic, sunlight reflected everywhere.

"Look! Marula Trees are growing out of the water," Abioye said, widening his eyes.

"They grow on top of each other, reaching for the roof of the cave there in the center," Yomí pointed.

"Are those docks?" Aamira asked as they turned a corner and saw wooden docks and hundreds of old ships tied up.

"There must be hundreds of ships down here that haven't been used in years," Adewara said.

The royal family and Adewara were able to dock their ship; surrounded by Marula Trees everywhere.

"Where do we go from here?" Abioye asked.

"We need to climb our way up these Marula Trees," Adewara said with his shoulders back. "It's the only way we can get to the city of Timbuktu."

"Grab your packs," Aamira ordered. "Everyone. The family and the sailors. No one gets left behind."

Rations were stuffed in backpacks as the group exited on the docks and set their sights toward the Marula trees piling one on top of the other in the center of the chasm. Sunlight shone bright from what looked like the exit to the cavern high above.

"I don't get it," Yinká said as he jumped onto the roots of a Marula that looked like they were growing directly from the branches of the tree beneath it.

"What don't you get, Little Brother?" Yekú asked, climbing behind him.

"These trees. It's like they've been stacked specifically for us to climb out of here. But they seem to be growing out of each other. Is this one tree, or a bunch of trees living symbiotically?"

"Does it matter?" Yemí questioned as he climbed.

The wind increased as they climbed. Several of the sailors fell to their deaths as they reached thousands of feet above the water below. Aamira kept her eyes on the bright light ahead, but realized they were pushing what remained of the boat crew too hard.

"They need to stop climbing," she shouted to Adewara. "We've already lost three men!"

"None of us can stop now!" Admiral Abdul urged. "These men are brave, as am I. We follow you to our deaths if necessary. Worry not for us, kings and queens of Sahael. We serve you now and forever!"

"Look, I see some ladders made out of wood with the Sahaelian Sigil of the Marula Tree inscribed on them," Abioye cried. He pointed toward the opening at the top of the cave. Indeed, ladders snaked down through the branches.

"We can take it to the surface of A.M.I.T," Adewara said.

The final climb up the ladders allowed the group to exit the cave. Aamira helped pull up the remaining sailors before looking around to see where they were. Trees grew around the hole they had just escaped, and through this grove, Aamira saw a city of pale stone glistening in the bright afternoon sunlight.

"Timbuktu," Adewara smiled.

Relief washed over Aamira. Her sons embraced and

cheered as Abioye wiped a tear from his eye. The months on the ocean had been trying in different ways than any of them had been used to. The constant fear of being discovered had weighed on all of them, but it lifted now like a fog.

Adewara led them toward the city, but before they had drawn within a half a mile, Aamira could tell something was wrong. No sound emanated from the beautiful place, no voices or music. Only the call of birds overhead evidenced any life at all in the area.

Her suspicions were confirmed as they took their first steps onto an empty cobblestone street.

"No one is here. Where is everyone?" Aamira asked.

"This place is utterly devoid of people," Abioye agreed.

"There must be an explanation for this," Yomí said, looking around.

A pained expression pressed Adewara's features toward his nose. "They must have gone into hiding after the downfall of Sahael." Adewara took a deep breath. "The intended purpose of Timbuktu was to empower and educate the Alkebulan people to know about their history. It was kept secret from witans who didn't share the same skin color as the Egyptians, Hornans, Sahaelians, and Alkebulans. Every Black person acquired knowledge and had access to it to enlighten their minds. Once it was learned, it never left their minds since they were all Alkebulan. When Sahael was invaded, the Narsans were able to find out the location of this place."

His voice echoed slightly in the silent city. A breeze blew down one of the corridors, tossing dried leaves around.

Adewara stood there for a moment as if trying to control his emotions. Aamira had no idea what he had expected to find here, but an empty city certainly didn't seem to be what he had anticipated. They had all given so much of themselves for the cause of reuniting their people, but Adewara was a student of Timbuktu. Seeing it in this abandoned state would be nothing short of torturous for the Educator.

Eventually, Adewara spoke again. "Those that lived in Timbuktu were forced into hiding and have chosen to remain in hiding until the time of restoration is completed." He looked around and scratched his head. "We need to get going; the Royal library isn't far. Maybe there will be some documents there that will shed light. Maybe."

The group walked slowly after that, making their way to the center of Timbuktu. Wooden shutters hung from the windows as rats scurried from house to house, oblivious to the visitors in their midst. They reached the royal library, a twenty-story building with a round roof made of polished stone. Pillars carved into the shape of animals and men held up the main floor. Adewara led them to the main entrance where a series of letters were etched into the stone above, reading S.T.E.A.H.M.

"There's an acronym at the top of the door," Aamira said, nodding her head toward the carving.

"Indeed, the same writing sits atop every single building entrance in Timbuktu," Adewara said.

"What does the name S.T.E.A.H.M mean?" Abioye asked.

"The acronym on the walls represents what is taught in the city of Timbuktu; ensuring that all Sahaelians and Alkebulans are continually educated in the ways of Aarde," Adewara said.

"Will you just tell us what the acronym means?" Yekú asked. "I'm hungry, and I know we never eat until you've spent an hour telling us something you think is important."

"It is important," Adewara snapped.

"Then tell us, already," Yinká smiled.

"What is taught here?" Aamira asked.

"H to understand the tactics of witan men and witan women and their racist nuances in every way," Adewara said, staring at the carving.

"What does the acronym stand for?" Aamira asked again, deepening her voice.

Adewara nodded as if suddenly understanding their impatience. "The letters represent Science, Technology, Engineering, Arts, Health, and Mathematics. This particular library houses all the knowledge and events that have ever happened in Aarde and that are currently happening now." Adewara's voice cracked slightly, emotion breaking through his tough exterior.

"How is it possible that the library could have current information if no one is here to record it?" Aamira asked.

"The responsible tribes have gone into willful exile," Adewara replied. "They left this place, but a few were sent into Aarde to help the gatherings take place."

"A few?" Abioye asked, gazing with focus at Adewara. "What does that mean?"

"Let us get inside before we ask any more questions," Adewara said, obviously not in the mood to deg deeper.

"How do we enter this place?" Yomí questioned as he stared at the statue of a man devouring a snake. "There are no doors; there are just solid steel walls that blend in with all of the buildings."

"If you four boys walk up to the wall, the eye of Horus will light up." Adewara pointed to the carving straight in front of them. "When that happens, your eyes will light up green." He turned to Aamira. "After the four of them do this, the large doors will appear and be opened permanently all over Timbuktu."

Just as Adewara spoke, the princes stood before the doors, and they appeared. The sound of stone scraping against stone echoed throughout the city. All doors had been opened.

"The ancients never do anything small, do they?" Abioye said, rubbing his eyes.

"The power of the Ancients is how this is possible," Adewara added. "Once the first gathering is complete, all of Sahael, the realms, and Alkebulan will have access to this knowledge in Timbuktu once again." Adewara waved the group forward. "Let us enter the library and see what we can learn."

CHAPTER X
TIMBUKTU

A.M.I.T. Timbuktu

The royal family, Adewara, and the five remaining sailors all entered the twenty-story library. Thousands of books lined the walls.

"There are four distinct areas in the great library," Adewara said as they walked up a flight of stairs to the second floor. "Each section is for the four the chosen bloodlines of Sahael.

Sapphire, Emerald, Hematite gray, and Turquoise accents lined specific shelves, matching the trim on each of the books in that section.

"If someone wanted to know more," Adewara continued as they walked, "they accessed the Nabtahenge gates and would have the library navigators and library gate guardians help get them to the correct locations in the ancient library. The Nabtahenge gates are not active because the first gathering has not been completed yet."

The royal family walked down the watcher halls and passed by a Nabta door that led them to Nephrophida's map room. It was where visitors could see an overview of the ancient library and all of Aarde.

Adewara pointed at the glowing map on the table, which was demarcated into four sections, matching the color-coded nature they had observed throughout the library. "The map shows you are not permitted into the sections of the other three houses."

Yomí pointed at the map. "The Orishan sigil is lit up, emanating its fierce sapphire colors. Our Yoruban sigil is lit up and active as well, but the other two sigils are still dormant. Why is that, and does it mean those areas can't be entered by those royal lines?"

"The library of the Ancients is available to all Sahaelians and Alkebulans to come and learn about the Ancient families of Sahael and the Kemites," Adewara answered. "Many come to learn about the watchers of the four realms and their responsibilities for protecting Aarde. As to why the other house symbols are not illuminated, I can only guess. Their awakenings may not have occurred yet."

Or perhaps my sisters are dead, Aamira thought to herself. She hadn't seen her cousins in many years. Oadira of the Orishan line had obviously accomplished something if her symbol was glowing in the library, but what did that mean for the others that theirs remained dormant?

"This place is incredible," one of the sailors said.

"This place is a threat to all witans," Yemí said softly.

The royal family and Adewara left Nephrophida's map room and made their way to the Yoruban wing of the library. They climbed thousands of steps, much to the exhaustion of the sailors. They finally reached the entrance with its large green sigil of the short-faced bear glowing brightly. They all wiped the sweat from their foreheads as they sat down to rest and catch their breath.

"Was this area ever cut off to the rest of Alkebulan?"

Aamira asked, clearing her throat.

Adewara shook his head. "No. Typically, this area is accessible to all, but after the fall of Sahael, to preserve the ancient knowledge and to protect the histories, mechanisms were put into place to prevent all except for the ancient bloodlines from accessing it. This is the Yoruban family's library. This library has everything about your people. Everything you thought was lost is all here. Everything about your mother and father and your births such as why did Ibeji choose to make you a female and your husband a male? Even against the wishes of the Alkebulan council that caused division within the families that trickled down into the four realms and forced them to look after their own bloodlines. It ultimately caused the ancient lineages to go their separate ways. Answers are here."

The boys started exploring, with Yekú running into the room a few minutes later to gush about how the larders were well stocked with dried food and grain. He immediately set out to make some bread in the kitchens if he could get the fires burning again. They would have a hot meal if it was the last thing he did. Admiral Abdul and his men were honored to help.

Adewara for his part walked throughout the library frantically, looking for the Yoruban tomes that were reserved for their bloodlines only. After searching for a few hours, Adewara found them.

"What is so important about these records?" Aamira asked as she sat next to him at one of the tables.

"The Yoruban tomes are magical," he replied, "keeping a constant recording of Yoruban history. You asked about how these records remain up to date when there is no one here to record. These records are linked to other records across Aarde that are kept to this very moment by Educators such as myself. They are always located in the personal quarters of the King and Queen Regent of the Yoruban bloodline."

Adewara scrolled through the hefty book and smiled broadly as he discovered the information he was seeking.

"What are you looking for?" Aamira asked, spying over Adewara's shoulder.

"It reads here that the Anunnaki went through all of Alkebulan looking for those who share their same bloodline," Adewara read. "The Chosen Bloodlines were responsible for helping establish the Empires of Kush, Axum, and Songhai after the eastern realms agreed to make Alkebulan the primary power in all of Aarde. The Anunnaki, Negralli, and the Negraté helped get the Empires of Kush, Axum, and Songhai be established. It says here that the Anunnaki bloodline was sent down by Ishtar and Obatala to preserve the Negrundians, a tribe of only men. Their sole purpose was to safeguard the realm's right to ensure that Alkebulans best interests were always looked after. However, when your grandmother fell in love with your grandfather, it defied realm law and the Sahaelian council's demands."

"Why was that such a big deal?" Aamira asked.

"Falling in love was not permitted. Their passion was upheld by Ishtar, Obatala, Kainoa and Kaimana however."

"You can't help who you love," Aamira said.

Adewara's dreadlock fell from his shoulder as he shook his head. "Love changed the parameters of their responsibilities, meaning they started to see the people as their own and started to look out for their own. As a result, both bloodlines merged, creating the Yoruban lineage. The melding of the two formed a unification for the benefit of Sahael. The safeguards were put in place by the four Kings and the four Queens with Solomon's help. The protections countered Lord Commander Natas' son Damien, who took control of Naharis's Realm and then transferred that power to his father who was able to gain control and influence over the witan power structure in western Aarde. The Narsans from the island of Narsa were witans who preferred isolation beyond the Nibiru wall, while the other nations in the east chose to look after Alkebulan. Narsa had its eyes on Western Aarde. After the Nibiru, had built the wall."

"The Nibiru wall?" Aamira asked,

"Yes. They were the great builders of bridges and walls throughout all of Aarde."

"When will we meet up with Solomon?" Aamira asked. It was a question she had held onto for some time, but now that they had made it to Timbuktu, it seemed the perfect time to bring it up.

Adewara stared at the large book in front of him. "No one really knows. Solomon has secretly remained in exile and has been giving orders and directives."

"Secretly remained in exile?" Abioye asked, running his hands through his braids. "Why would he do that? He's powerful right? Natas is afraid of him, isn't he?"

"That is a conversation for another day; let us focus on the task at hand," Adewara said, looking at the tomes.

"Why can't we have this conversation now?" Aamira asked, feeling her heart beat a bit faster. Here they were in the library of Timbuktu, but Adewara still held back details from them.

"Patience is needed, Empress."

"I've shown plenty of patience, Adewara. I'm just sick of being drip-fed information; information we need in order to succeed in our mission."

Aamira stood and looked back toward the stairs. She felt the truth of something in that moment and needed to voice it. Would Adewara confirm her suspicions or deflect like he always did when not wanting to answer a direct question?

"Oadira's been here, hasn't she?" Aamira asked. Tears came to her eyes as she spoke. The fact that the Orishan symbol was illuminated on the map like the Yoruban sign acted as confirmation to her thoughts.

Adewara tapped his finger slowly on the leather pages of the book. Tears came to his eyes as well.

"Yes," he said, voice hoarse.

Abioye stood and hugged Aamira. He looked over at Adewara. "When? How long ago?"

"Weeks. Perhaps only a few days."

"Where did they go?" Abioye asked, still embracing his wife. Can we track them down? Can we catch up with them?"

Adewara wiped his tears and sat up straighter. "I doubt it. I would assume they were able to somehow get the gates to work and traveled via portal. I would have loved to see…them."

"So, my sisters at one point or another will make their way here?" Aamira asked.

"Indeed," Adewara said.

"Perhaps we should just wait until the others arrive," Abioye said.

"No, we have our purpose, and they have theirs," Adewara said.

Wait," Aamira said, pulling away from Abioye and stepping closer to Adewara. "You've never met Oadira."

"Correct."

"Then why are you getting so emotional? Someone else is with them that you do know. Am I right?"

Adewara closed his eyes. "Yes. They are traveling with an

Educator by the name of Lyshyla. I have not seen her in many years. She is…very competent.”

Very competent? What was Adewara hiding? Aamira would not let it go.

“Who is this woman?” Aamira pressed.

“An Educator.”

“Why is she special to you?”

“She’s not.”

“She is! She’s more important to you than Oadira. I can hear it in your voice.”

Adewara stood and slammed the book closed. “I will not answer any more questions in this vein. I am a servant of Solomon, nothing more.”

Aamira stood in front of him, tall and powerful. “You love this woman; this Lyshyla. Answer me! Tell me the truth or leave!”

A great pain seemed to claw at Adewara’s chest. Despite his efforts to deny Aamira’s words, his body language betrayed the truth. Whoever this Lyshyla was, he loved her deeply.

“You do love her.”

“It is…unimportant.”

Aamira grabbed Adewara’s shoulders and shook the man. “Tell me the truth! Tell me something real!”

“She…is my wife,” Adewara whispered, barely audible. “And I will speak no more of it until Sahael is once more redeemed.”

The Educator turned and walked out, leaving Aamira and Abioye alone.

Shock rippled up Aamira’s spine. She had known Adewara since her first day arriving in the Sand Lands of IFF. He had been her counselor and friend. Despite his penchant for holding onto information, she never would have guessed he would hide such an important aspect of his life from her. She wanted to hit him and rage against him. For Educators, what remained unsaid was always as important as what was spoken. In this case, a key truth had been omitted that built a wall instantly as far as Aamira was concerned. His silence on something so important was as real as if Adewara had lied to her all these years.

How could he not tell her he had a wife? How could he not tell her boys? What other key secrets was he keeping? What other lies of omission did he harbor?

If her sons ever learned of this, they would be devastated. They would see themselves through Adewara's eyes, as nothing more than tools to be used and discarded.

"What are you thinking?" Abioye asked as a breeze blew through the library windows.

"That I hate Educators."

"I'm being serious," Abioye smiled.

Aamira turned to him, fists tight. "So am I."

Over the next few days, Adewara seemed to avoid the others, spending most of his time in other areas of the library while Aamira and the family remained in the Yoruban section. Yekú had spent most of his time in the kitchens making different meals to their delight. He had become quite the cook, and Aamira was only now appreciating his talents.

On the second day in the library, Aamira found a book with the seal of the Orishan line on it. Wanting to feel closer to her cousin Oadira, she and Abioye had begun reading it together. They would lie on a couch with Aamira pressed back into Abioye's chest. Wind would blow through the windows and birds would occasionally fly into the library before squawking their farewells.

"The Negralli and the Nephilim merged and created the Orisha bloodline," Abioye said, pointing at a pedigree chart on one of the interior pages. "It says their men and boys were all killed when they arrived in Nyathera's asteroid that hit in the middle of Alkebulan and created Sahael."

"Keep reading," Aamira smiled as she snuggled against her husband.

"Lord Lieutenant Damien had all the boys and men killed," Abioye continued, "preventing them from multiplying. The Lord Lieutenant appeared with the Nethanites as they emerged from Nyathera's, killing the men and boys. After not seeing anymore, the Lord Lieutenant left thinking they were all dead."

"You know what's interesting?" Aamira asked as she pulled the book from Abioye's hands.

"What?"

"Here in the back, it lists the Educators who contributed to the history of that particular book. These records were written by Solomon, Lyshyla, Abdul, and Adewara," Aamira said.

"Yes," a voice echoed in the large open room. Adewara strode forward, hands behind his back. "What you're reading are the events that were done by the four of us and the Educators in Timbuktu to ensure the bloodlines were established; a story for another day."

"Aren't they all?" Aamira said snidely. She sat up away from Abioye and pointed at the book. "It says here that Ninqi of the Nephilim married in secret Nergal of the Negralli, melding the bloodlines of an all-female lineage with males. It was done out of necessity and survival, creating division between the other three realms. The Watcher council in Horn found out about the secret marriages of Nergal of the Negralli, and Ninqi of the Nephilim. The leaders of the people of Horn were so incensed, they banned Nier's realm. As a result, it forced the other realms to do the same thing, forcing all four realms to break up as a result."

"That is correct," Adewara nodded. "Horn countered by cutting off all contact to each of the four realms. As a result, this closed the Alkebulans off from magic, long life, and spiritual guidance from the four realms."

Adewara sat across from the emperor and empress, fiddling with the cover of a nearby book. The echo of bird song flitted through the windows.

"I am…sorry I never told you about Lyshyla." Adewara spoke quietly; deliberately. "The thought of her brings great…pain to me. Your family has sacrificed much, but you must understand that many of us have made sacrifices that cut to the very marrow. I look forward to a day of unification for all people when I will see and embrace my love again. Until that time, please do not make me relive my pain. I would not have it spoken of again. If you have ever respected me, please respect this."

Aamira stood and put her hand on Adewara's shoulder. "I respect you, Adewara. You can be frustrating at times, but I never once doubted your commitment to the salvation of our people. Knowing your pain only fortifies that surety. I'm just sorry you must suffer so."

"To live is to suffer," Adewara nodded. He then looked up into Aamira's eyes. "But to live is also to have joy. Both have their season. My season of joy will be bountiful, I have no doubt."

"What will you tell the princess?" Aamira asked.

"Nothing. They needn't know."

"If they ever find out, they'll hate you for it. To hide something so intimate from men who see you as a mentor will be devastating for them. They'll think you don't trust them, or worse, don't care about them."

Adewara turned to leave. "They will understand. And if they don't, it won't matter so long as they redeem Sahael."

That night over dinner, the discussion circled to the next steps on their journey. The group sat on a tenth story balcony surrounded by candelabras overlooking the empty city of Timbuktu. The wind blew cool as the sun set. The sailors had left the royal family to eat their dinner of Yekú's fresh bread and platters of sun-dried fruits and meats privately, much to Aamira's gratitude. Much of the business needing to be discussed was family business, and she needed to be able to speak freely.

"How do we get the gates open?" she asked between bites. "Oadira got them to work, and there is still energy there in the rocks on the roof of the library."

"We have no navigator," Adewara chewed. "Energy or not, without the proper knowledge, there is little any of us can do. Oadira, and whoever she had with her, must have included a navigator."

"Where do we find one?" Aamira asked.

Adewara shrugged and motioned toward the empty city

below as if pointing out their predicament.

"What about the other Royal Families? What role did they all play in this?" Yekú asked as he spread warm fruit preserve on a piece of bread. "If Mom's cousin was here even recently, and the gates on the top floor are still crackling with energy, what does that mean for us?"

"It means that the path is closed, but can be opened," Adewara replied.

Yinká turned to Adewara. "Was Timbuktu ever accessible to all Aardians to take part in the vast knowledge stored in the ancient libraries?"

"No," Adewara confirmed. "Witans were forbidden to have access to this knowledge. They have a predisposition to evil with this type of knowledge. They'd try to spread witan supremacy over Aarde. There are powers here that many of them would use to manipulate, enslave, and control the Blacks in Aarde in every feasible way. This is why Lord Commander Natas and the Narsans have chosen to live on the opposite side of the Nibiru wall."

"So, Lord Commander Natas was allowed to live how and where he wanted without any supervision?" Yemí asked between bites of dried jerky.

"Without the help of Horn, we were unable to track Lord Commander Natas and his son Lord Lieutenant Damien," Adewara explained.

"Basically, a witan fascist regime was allowed to grow and take hold," Abioye said, munching some grains. "They've now become a threat to all Black people in Aarde."

"Who are these witans?" Aamira asked.

"The Narsans are the witans who invaded Sahael, destroyed three of the four cities, Khartoum palace, and dispersed the four bloodlines, enslaving the Alkebulans," Adewara said.

"How can we find out what these witans are doing in Western Aarde?" Yemí questioned.

Adewara shrugged and tossed a few nuts in his mouth. "We don't really know. My order has been trying to find out for years but have not been able to find anything. I know you all have questions that require explanations. I assure you; you'll find those answers here. Those questions that you don't find answers to, you'll have to wait until you get to Sahael. And that's not just me being an Educator who holds back information." He smiled playfully. "That is simply the truth. Not all knowledge can be understood until the right moment, even if you have all the data right before your eyes."

Yinká looked from left to right and finished chewing his food. "I have a question, Adewara."

"Feel free to ask it, my future High King."

"I was in a lower level of the library today and I came across a series of white books with the symbol of the sphinx lion's head on the cover of the books. What does the symbol mean?"

Adewara took a deep breath. "This sigil represents the Egyptians. You saw a large sigil circle of four large lions devouring the back end of each other forming a circle. The sphinx lion's head is in the center of the ring of lions."

"Yes," Yinká nodded. "The lions had different-colored eyes that resembled the eyes of the four bloodlines."

"The Rysallians were influenced by Lord Commander Natas, who used them to infect and create the Trinity," Adewara said. "I'm convinced this is why the war in Katunkumene happened. After losing the Katunkumean war, Lord Commander Natas was cast out of his father and mother's presence," Adewara read.

"They cast out their own son?" Yinká asked.

"Yes, Lord Commander Natas was sent to the Nothing in the outer Realm of Darkness. No pity was taken on him until he regained entry into Aarde through his son Damien. Lord Lieutenant Damien was sent down with the chosen bloodlines and then kicked out of Timbuktu university. He ventured west and eventually took control of Naharis's Realm. Afterwards Lord Commander Natas capitalized on the anger of the Rysallians for feeling betrayed by the chosen bloodlines. The Rysallians didn't realize they were lied to and were forced to believe that they were rejected by the other five tribes from Lord Commander Natas, who knew about their weaknesses."

Aamira pushed her plate away. "Lord Commander Natas used their discontent and turned it into anger, resentment, and entitlement. I saw it all the time during my youth in the colonies. People who had no right to feel slighted would become so enraged at their perceived injustices that they would kill innocent people and think they were doing God's work."

"Lord Commander Natas convinced the Rysallians they were the chosen people and were isolated for their own personal gain to learn the ways of Aarde," Adewara confirmed. "They could then subject their Imperial rule and judgments to anyone they deemed their inferiors. The Trinity was created by Lord Commander Natas to help invade, control, and rebuild the old world in his image."

Yinká picked up a dried strawberry and examined it closely. "I should read those books, shouldn't I?"

"Yes," Adewara answered. "All of you need to know these details. Some of it I have taught you already through the years, but details will resonate now more clearly for you since you have seen death and the oppression of your people. I was angry at first when I heard you had snuck out of the inn to follow the children of

Ikegwuru, but now I know that was a blessing. You saw with your own eyes what your people suffer. It is easy to turn a blind eye to pain when it is far away. You have seen it close up. Now is the time to read and understand. Know this: Lord Commander Natas sent messengers into Western lands to infiltrate for several years. His messengers created dirt roads to create routes for trade, enabling the Trinity to send out missionaries and merchants throughout the old world. They became friendly with The Arth Nations, The States of 'Or and The divided D.I.M.-T.I.M. Lands. The D.I.M. Nations were constantly at war with the Rysallians, but being merchants and messengers for Lord Commander Natas, the D.I.M. allowed them to create maps and gain access to routes. After years of fighting, Lord Commander Natas and the Trinity approached the Rysallians, who were overcome with joy. They were ideally spread throughout the old world, fighting to acquire a way of life. They felt that they were robbed of their birthright."

"I remember this lesson from our youth," Yomí said.

"Indeed," Adewara said. "If you keep studying, you will learn deeper truths, like that Lord Commander Natas told them everything they wanted to hear; promising them they'd regain their stature within Western Aarde. The Rysallians quickly jumped at the opportunity. The trinity provided a home for the Rysallians, and the loyalty and deception of dominating Western Aarde. Lord Commander Natas told the Rysallians they were the original people, and they should show and exert their dominance in Aarde."

"What made these Rysallians different from the six scared bloodlines?" Prince Yomí asked.

Adewara took a piece of bread and chewed it thoughtfully. "They were the only witan bloodline persuaded and convinced that they had been ostracized and rejected by the other five bloodlines. Lord Commander Natas, in disguise, convinced them that they should get their revenge on the five different bloodlines. The

Rysallians merged with the Trinity, mingling bloodlines, and sharing their powers, gifts, and abilities with those of Lord Commander Natas' choosing."

"Why would they follow such a lunatic?" Yemí asked.

"Lord Commander Natas was able to control death by giving them eternal life, unlike the other five tribes. The Rysallians would have the ability to use the dark artes," Adewara said.

"This is why they were influential merchants and traders, isn't it?" Yekú said.

"The witan bloodline was the only bloodline with the power of Echolocation," Adewara continued, finishing his bread. "This Arte gave them the ability to locate anyone they desired, no matter where they were. Tens of thousands of our brothers died in the first few years of the Rysallian expansion alone."

"All because of a lie," Yinká said, shaking his head.

"They believe the lie," Aamira added. Her years growing up on the plantation has taught her about the power of deception, particularly when employed by powerful witans. "It's their belief that has become so dangerous. They slaughter and enslave thinking they are justified. Such things are always wicked. In the end, they will know the truth, but by then, they will already have destroyed themselves."

"Lies are potent when people want to believe them in place of the truth," Adewara agreed. "Lord Commander Natas understood this, which is why he wanted to manipulate the witan bloodline and merge it with the trinity bloodlines in Western Aarde. Over 100 years ago, the Rysallian merged bloodlines in secret."

"It would now appear that Lord Commander Natas has the power to control the Rysallian bloodline," Yinká said.

"Indeed, Natas controls the bloodline, using it to invade the lands in Western Aarde with the Narsans. The Narsans took all the resources for themselves and tamed Western lands. Rather than enslaving the inhabitants, they were incorporated into the service of their country. They were drafted into the Trinity armies, and T.I.M. became a Trinity stronghold. He had fully converted the Trinity to his religion. They were now following the edicts he had issued, so that they could all rise once again in Damien's presence. Natas wanted to show his father and mother that his plan should have been accepted before the civil war that led to his banishment into outer realms of darkness."

"This was all to prove his parents wrong?" Yinká asked.

"Listen to me on this," Adewara said. "Lord Commander Natas believed he could save all his brothers and sisters and wanted to show his love for them by providing a way they could all return to Katunkumene. As wicked and evil as he has become, his initial reasoning came down to love."

Aamira sat back, feeling her body warm with anger. "He loves nothing. Natas is evil incarnate."

"And what are you capable of when love is the focus, Empress Aamira?" Adewara asked. He threw a dried date into his mouth as Aamira fumed.

"I am capable of much," she replied evenly.

"Of course you are," Adewara nodded. "Love is a powerful thing. What Natas is and what he was are two different things. Never forget, any of you, that love can lead to as much suffering as hate. You must control your emotions and your pride if you hope to bring peace to these lands. Lord Commander Natas would make a return to Ishtar and Obatala possible by taking away the free will of his brothers and sisters. Free will; the right to choose for themselves. All our spirit brothers and sisters would have to follow a set of stringent, rigid rules requiring them to live a specific way, ensuring Lord Commander had full control to ensure no mistakes were made. After it's all been established and done, Natas' plan ensures that only he has power over death enabling nightfall to come to pass."

The family sat silently after that, eating their food as the candles flickered in the wind. Aamira had never thought of Natas being motivated by anything beyond selfish hate.

Love? Was the demon man even capable of such deep emotion?

And yet, what had Aamira done in the name of love? She had killed. She had maimed. She had faced monsters. She had led armies in the name of love.

Was she really so different from Natas at the end of the day?

She shook her head. *Yes, I'm different than him. Where he brings oppression, I will bring safety. Where he conquers, I will liberate.*

Aamira smiled. Wherever their path led from here, one day she would look at Natas as he breathed his last and it would not be love that she felt for him.

Was he capable of love? It didn't matter so long as he was capable of death and damnation.

She would make sure he suffered both.

[To be continued in Volume 2 Book 4]